# MURDER, STAGE LEFT

# MURDER, STAGE LEFT

A Nero Wolfe Mystery

*Robert Goldsborough*

MYSTERIOUSPRESS.COM

OPEN ROAD
INTEGRATED MEDIA
NEW YORK

Cover design by Olivia Brodtman

Author photo by Colleen Berg

ISBN 978-1-5040-4111-9

Published in 2017 by MysteriousPress.com/Open Road Integrated Media, Inc.
180 Maiden Lane
New York, NY 10038
www.mysteriouspress.com
www.openroadmedia.com

*To Otto Penzler,*

*Publisher and editor extraordinaire,*

*for his continuing support and encouragement*

# MURDER, STAGE LEFT

# CHAPTER 1

The reviewers at the *Times*, *News*, *Post*, and *Gazette* all had called it the "non-musical hit of the season," or words to that effect, and as I sat that August night in the sold-out Belgrave Theater on West Forty-Fourth Street during the first act of *Death at Cresthaven*, I wondered what I was missing that those esteemed scribes from the daily papers had seen.

The drama, set sometime before World War II in the faded parlor of a Connecticut mansion whose best days were behind it, chronicled a family in decline, both financially and psychologically. At the center of the performance was Marjorie Mills, the tall and elegant grande dame of the household, portrayed as a woman in denial by longtime Broadway fixture Ashley Williston.

Lily Rowan, seated on my left, seemed more involved in the action on the stage than I, and at an intermission in the lobby, I asked her why.

"I thought that you, of all people, would enjoy a good mystery, Escamillo," she said, using the nickname she had tagged me with years ago after I had a run-in with an angry bull in an Upstate pasture. "The acting is really quite good—even Ashley Williston, who I know casually and who I've always thought tended to ham it up both onstage and off."

"Well, I will withhold judgment until the final curtain falls, but for the moment, mark me down as underwhelmed. By the way, how is it that you happen to know the famous Miss Williston?"

"'Know' may be overstating the relationship, but I have met Ashley on more than one occasion," Lily said as we shared a candy bar. "She entertained us with some monologues from her performances at a benefit banquet for an orphanage where I serve on the board, which was very generous of her. And we were seated side by side at a luncheon at the Plaza a year or so ago for a 'send a city kid to summer camp' program. But I have to say that a little bit of Ashley goes a long way."

"How so?"

"The woman is always performing. Even in casual one-on-one conversations, she sounds like she is directing her pear-shaped tones to a theatergoer in the back row of the balcony. I almost felt like I should applaud after one of her pronouncements. And of course everyone around us at the luncheon was constantly turning our way when she spoke. Not because the woman had something interesting to say—she didn't—but because you could hear her throughout the room. And it was a large room."

"Not how I would choose to spend a meal," I said.

"Nor I. But in a way, I do feel a certain sympathy for the woman. It is an open secret in the theater community that it galls her she has never won a Tony Award over her long career."

"Based on what you have said about her work, it seems like there is a reason for that."

Lily nodded. "Ashley has been one of the featured players in God knows how many Broadway dramatic productions, about four or five of which I've seen, and her notices have been lukewarm at best. The best way to summarize the reviewers' rap against her is that 'she tries too hard.'"

"How have the critics treated her in this play?"

"Kindly, overall. If I were to predict, I would say she really feels she's finally got a fair chance at that elusive Tony."

My opinion of the play, and of Ashley Williston, improved somewhat during the second and third acts, although—as the drama of a fractured and down-at-the-heels family, set in a timeworn Connecticut country estate—the production was only fair. But the audience seemed to eat it up, particularly the surprise ending, and the cast got a long and largely standing ovation.

"Well, Archie, what is your verdict now?" Lily asked as we devoured a late supper at Rusterman's Restaurant—for my money, the best eatery in Manhattan outside of the brownstone where I live.

"It was not the best night I've ever spent in a Broadway theater, but it was far from the worst, and Miss Williston did seem to hold up her end of the proceedings relatively well after all," I said. "Besides, no one has ever asked me to be a theater critic, so I am hardly qualified to judge the production." I figured those were to be my last words and last thoughts concerning *Death at Cresthaven* and Ashley Williston. Just goes to show how wrong one can be.

# CHAPTER 2

The next four days are not worth wasting many words on in these pages, except to report that Nero Wolfe—with some help from me—wrapped up a forgery case for a Madison Avenue fine-art dealer that involved a phony Rembrandt portrait—a very good phony, at that. The result was the forger's arrest and a fine payday for us, pushing our bank balance to a level where Wolfe could, for months, concentrate totally on the things he enjoys most: his ten thousand orchids; gourmet meals prepared by live-in Swiss chef Fritz Brenner; the reading of up to three books simultaneously; the London *Times* and *New York Times* crossword puzzles; and, of course, the consumption of Remmers beer, which Fritz orders by the case.

That Thursday morning at nine thirty, I was at my desk typing up correspondence dictated by my boss to an orchid fancier in Florida when the phone rang. "Nero Wolfe's office,

Archie Goodwin speaking," I answered, as I always do during working hours.

"Ah, yes, Mr. Goodwin, I was confident I would find you on the job. Of course I know where Mr. Wolfe is at this moment," the caller said, chuckling. I recognized the voice of Lewis Hewitt, a longtime acquaintance and occasional dinner guest at Wolfe's table, as well as a world-class orchid grower and a multimillionaire who owns a sprawling estate on Long Island.

"Yes, Mr. Hewitt, you do, of course, know his schedule as well as I do: four hours a day, nine to eleven in the morning and four to six before dinner, nursing those orchids up in the plant rooms on the fourth floor, plant rooms you have visited many times. Can I give him a message?"

"You certainly can, sir. I have a friend, a very good friend, named Roy Breckenridge. You may have heard of him."

I had heard of him, but I was not about to interrupt Hewitt, whom I knew liked the sound of his own resonant voice. "Go on," I said.

"You may be aware that Mr. Breckenridge currently is producing a hit drama on Broadway, *Death at Cresthaven*."

"I believe I've heard something about it."

"I'm sure you have, and this is the reason for my call. Mr. Breckenridge is terribly concerned about his play."

"Bad reviews, eh?" I posed, knowing that was not the case.

"Far from it. In fact, the reviews have been close to stellar. One of the local critics even called it 'the best drama about a decadent and dysfunctional family since Lillian Hellman's *The Little Foxes*.'"

"Then what's the problem?" I asked, trying to keep the irritation out of my voice.

"Roy Breckenridge is an extremely perceptive man. He tells

me he senses trouble ahead, big trouble, and he wants to discuss it with Nero Wolfe."

"Can you be more specific?"

For at least a half minute, I got no reply. Finally, Hewitt spoke. "I have known Roy for more than twenty years, and I have never seen him more agitated. He has this . . . feeling, sensation, call it what you will . . . that something dire is going to happen involving his play or possibly himself. I did press him for specifics, but he chose not to discuss it with me.

"He knows Nero Wolfe and I are friends, and he asked—pleaded, really—for me to set up an appointment for him to see your boss. You have got a lot of influence with Wolfe. I am sure you can persuade him to see Roy."

"You overstate my influence, I assure you," I told Hewitt. "The man I work for does exactly what he wants to do and nothing more. I've run up against a stone wall with him more times than I can begin to count."

"Perhaps I can help you persuade him to see Roy. Speak these words to him: *Grammangis spectabilis.*"

"Can you spell that?" He did, and I dutifully entered the words in my notebook.

Some background on Lewis Hewitt: I have mentioned that he, like Wolfe, is an orchid fancier of the first order; that he is rich, very rich; and that he has often dined with us, one of the few people to get periodic invitations. Hewitt is as outgoing as Wolfe is reclusive. Where my boss's idea of a daring venture is his twice-monthly ten-block trip from the old brownstone on West Thirty-Fifth Street in Manhattan to his barber, with me playing chauffeur, Lewis Hewitt travels the world at least twice a year in search of exotic orchids, of which he has a collection that equals Wolfe's.

He also makes frequent visits to the opera, the symphony,

museum openings, and benefit dinners. In the society pages of the New York papers, he has been described as a *bon vivant*, a *boulevardier*, and in plainer terms, "a man about town." Hewitt's wealth is inherited, as is his sprawling estate on Long Island, but to his credit, he has spread much of his dough around to numerous charitable institutions and causes, so his generosity is not in question.

To say that he and Wolfe are competitive when it comes to their quest for exotic orchids would be a gross understatement. Each has, on occasion, possessed a rare species that the other has coveted, and over the years, a good deal of horse trading has taken place between them, along with some tension. Overall, however, their relations have been cordial. Each dines at the other's home at least once a year, so Wolfe's forays out to Long Island, with me again as chauffeur, are among his other rare ventures from the brownstone.

Despite the fact that I have been entering pollination records onto cards for the files for years, I by no means qualify as an expert on orchids, but I do know enough to realize that the two words I got from Hewitt had to do with an orchid, and in all likelihood, a rare one. It would be interesting to see Wolfe's reaction both to Hewitt's request and to those words.

I heard the whir of the elevator, and at one minute after eleven, Wolfe strode into the office, placed a raceme of purple orchids in the vase on his desk, and settled into the reinforced chair built to accommodate his seventh of a ton.

"Good morning, Archie, did you sleep well?" he asked, as he always does, then rang for beer as he always does.

"I did sleep well, after I got over losing the biggest pot of the game at Saul Panzer's poker table last night. But after all, it's only money. Easy come, easy go, or so they say."

Wolfe shrugged, indicating his lack of concern at my plight, and opened the first of two chilled bottles of beer Fritz Brenner had brought in on a tray with a glass, then turned to the letters I had stacked on his desk blotter.

"Before you start signing those, I should tell you about a call that came while you were up on the roof playing with your posies."

He looked up, irritated. "Yes?"

"Lewis Hewitt sends his regards. He also has an acquaintance who wants very much to meet with you."

"Flummery!"

"No sir, not flummery. The individual in question is Roy Breckenridge, a well-known and successful Broadway producer. Mr. Breckenridge seems to have a sense of foreboding about something to do with his current play, *Death at Cresthaven*."

"You saw the play with Miss Rowan, and it did not impress you."

"Correct, although, as I told her, I hardly qualify as a theater critic. And the production did seem to improve in the later acts."

"No matter. Tell Mr. Hewitt I am presently immersed in other projects and will be unable to see Mr. Breckenridge."

"I said to him that you probably would not be interested in seeing the producer, and he told me to say these words to you: *Grammangis spectabilis*."

Wolfe set his beer glass down hard and came forward in his chair, scowling. "What else did he say?"

"That is all. Am I to assume he is referring to some sort of orchid?"

"Some sort of orchid indeed," Wolfe snapped. "Confound it, he got them."

"Care to tell me what this is about?"

"*Grammangis spectabilis* is one of the rarest orchids in the world, and it is found only in Madagascar, where it recently was discovered. In the last few months, Mr. Hewitt traveled to Madagascar, which I see is not a coincidence."

"I admit I am sometimes slow, but I get the drift. Hewitt now has one or more of these orchids, and you don't."

Wolfe made a sound that roughly translated as "*Grrr.*"

"But," I continued, "Mr. Hewitt proposes a quid pro quo. You meet with Breckenridge and hear him out, and you get one of the Madagascar beauties—at least I assume they are beautiful."

"Blatant bribery!" Wolfe glared at his beer as if blaming it for the pickle he felt he was in. "To think he would stoop to this."

"I really do not see the problem," I said. "I realize our bank balance is healthy, but we both know how fast it can be depleted, given the cost of running this operation. Why not see Breckenridge? Surely, he can afford your rates."

Wolfe hates to work and always has. One of the reasons he hired me all those years ago was because he needed someone to goad him into action. It is not the part of the job that I relish most, but it may be the most important. I sat at my desk watching Wolfe stew. Finally, when he was halfway through his second beer, he drew in a bushel of air, exhaled, and said, "Call Mr. Hewitt and tell him I will see his friend tomorrow morning at eleven."

"Would you like to talk to Hewitt yourself?"

"I would not."

Lewis Hewitt's telephone number happens to be among several I know by heart. As I dialed it, Wolfe rose and marched off to the kitchen, undoubtedly to monitor Fritz's progress on the broiled shad *aux fines herbes* we would be having for lunch.

The phone rang once. "Hewitt speaking."

"Archie Goodwin here. Mr. Wolfe will see Mr. Breckenridge tomorrow morning at eleven."

"I knew you would be able to prevail upon him," he said with a chuckle. "I will call Roy and see if that time is convenient for him. He is a busy man."

"If he wants to see Nero Wolfe badly enough, he had better clear the time—period. Mr. Wolfe also happens to be busy. We are, at present, working on two cases simultaneously," I improvised.

"Very well. I will telephone you to confirm Mr. Breckenridge's appearance." Fifteen minutes later, Hewitt called to say the producer would come to the brownstone at the appointed time.

I went to the kitchen to inform Wolfe, and he nodded. "Archie, would you say our account with Mr. Cohen is in balance?" He was asking about Lon Cohen of the *New York Gazette*, a longtime friend who has supplied us with valuable information about a variety of people and events over the years. We, in turn, have delivered numerous scoops to him concerning cases we have worked on and that Wolfe has solved.

"I would say that, if anything, Lon owes us."

"That also is my impression. Telephone Mr. Cohen and find out what he knows about Mr. Breckenridge," Wolfe said, turning back to offer advice and counsel to Fritz, who was preparing the broiled shad.

Lon Cohen does not have a title I am aware of at the *Gazette*, the fifth-largest newspaper in America, but he has an office on the building's twentieth floor, three doors down from the publisher and with a dandy view of the Chrysler Building. I went back to my desk and dialed his number. He answered on the second ring.

"Hello, oh chronicler of the news in our fair land's largest metropolis. Can you spare a moment for an old friend?"

"The words 'old friend' always make me nervous when they come from you," Lon shot back. "Why do I get the feeling that I am about to have the touch put on me?"

"I will answer that by asking you a question Mr. Wolfe posed to me just moments ago: On balance, how is our account?"

A pause at the other end, which is rare for the voluble newsman. "As much as it pains me to say it, I am in your debt."

"Being in our debt should hardly pain you, especially given a couple of dandy scoops we've thrown to your rag in the last few months."

"Rag, indeed! You have cut me to the quick."

"No doubt, but I suspect that cut will heal quickly. Mr. Wolfe needs some information."

"I thought as much. Who or what does he want to know about?"

"It happens to be who—Roy Breckenridge."

"Ah, the noted impresario, whom the *Times* has dubbed the 'Baron of Broadway.' Is he a client of yours, and if so, why?"

"Not so fast, typewriter jockey; as usual, you are getting ahead of yourself. It is much too early to answer questions."

"Somehow, I have the feeling I've heard that line before. What, specifically, does your boss want to know?"

"Anything and everything."

"Well, thanks so much for getting specific. I will get back to you later, after I have talked to some people who know more about Breckenridge than I do. Of course, I'm sure you're in a hurry for this intelligence report."

"You are correct," I told him. "I eagerly await your call."

As it turned out, I did not have to do much waiting. Lon got back to me less than a half hour later.

"Here's what our drama critics and columnists have told me about Breckenridge," he said. "He is considered to be the savviest producer on Broadway right now, and close to being the best director as well. His productions have won a pile of Tonys over the years, in damned near every category: Best Director (himself, or course), Best Play, Best Musical, Best Revival of a Play, Best Performances by an Actor and an Actress, and on and on. I am sure you've heard of him, with all the plays you go to with Lily Rowan."

"I never pay attention to who the director is, or the producer, for that matter. When I go to the theater, which admittedly is not often, I am more interested in who's in the cast."

"Okay. Anyway, I am told Breckenridge never has any trouble getting the finances for one of his productions. His name is like gold to investors, including Wolfe's friend Lewis Hewitt, and he is generally well liked by cast members and staff, although he expects a lot out of his performers. The word 'perfectionist' gets used a lot in describing him.

"As to his personal life, Breckenridge has been married and divorced three times, no children. He is quite the man about town, often seen in the best restaurants and at parties with extremely attractive women, many of them decades younger than he. And in the last few years, his name has been linked to everyone from wealthy widows to stage and screen actresses, as well as to the daughter of a Greek shipping tycoon who is worth billions."

"Breckenridge sounds a little like the aforementioned Lewis Hewitt in his expensive tastes, although Hewitt has only been married once, and that union has lasted at least thirty years. Did you dig up any dirt on the producer?"

"Negative. If he has been up to any kind of skulduggery, nobody at the paper has unearthed it. And before you ask, he has never been a respondent in a paternity suit."

"I wasn't going to ask," I said in what I hoped was a hurt tone. "And I like the word 'skulduggery.' I haven't heard it in years."

"I've got a way with words, Archie. That's part of the reason they keep me around here and pay me the so-called big bucks."

"So that's your secret. Well, thanks for the information."

"Just remember where you heard it, in case . . . something comes up that might interest readers of the *Gazette*."

I told Lon I would remember and, after hanging up, went to the kitchen, where Wolfe and Fritz were in a heated discussion over the amounts of chives, chervil, and shallots that should be used in the shad roe entree. I didn't hang around to find out who was arguing which side of the issue. Arguments about food invariably bore me. I am more into consumption.

Because business is forbidden at lunch, I waited until Wolfe and I were back in the office with coffee before giving him the particulars on Breckenridge, but he did not seem overly interested, so I left him to peruse an orchid magazine and took a stroll in the summer sunshine.

# CHAPTER 3

The next day, Wolfe had barely gotten settled in the office after his morning session with the orchids when the doorbell rang. I walked down the hall to the front door, and through the one-way glass, I saw a tall, barrel-chested figure clad in a black homburg and black cashmere overcoat, even though the temperature did not warrant it.

"Good morning," I said, swinging open the door with a grin. "Mr. Breckenridge, I presume."

"And Mr. Goodwin, I also presume," he riposted, smiling. "So nice of Nero Wolfe to see me." He was an impressive specimen in his early sixties, at least six feet three, with piercing blue eyes and the ruddy cheeks of a man who probably liked his drink. I helped him off with his coat and admired the tailored gray pin-striped suit that must have cost more than most working stiffs earn in a month or two.

I steered Breckenridge down the hall to the office, introduced him to Wolfe, and directed him to the red leather chair. Apparently, our guest had been cued by Hewitt about Wolfe's distaste for shaking hands, because he did not offer a paw to his host.

"Thank you for agreeing to see me, Mr. Wolfe," he said, running a hand over well- barbered silver-gray hair. "I appreciate that your time is valuable."

Wolfe dipped his chin half an inch. "Can we offer you something to drink, sir? As you see, I am having beer."

"A Bloody Mary would be most welcome," he said. I went to the kitchen for a glass, ice, and tomato juice. Returning, I mixed the drink at the bar cart against one wall of the office as Breckenridge was speaking.

". . . so Lewis and I have been friends for many years, and he has very generously backed several of my plays."

"Just so," Wolfe said. "Mr. Hewitt tells us you have serious concerns about your current production."

"I do," Breckenridge said, nodding his thanks to me for the drink and crossing one leg over the other. "Lest you think me paranoid, I have been in this business for more than twenty years, and never have I had the uneasy feelings I do about *Death at Cresthaven*."

"The play has received positive reviews," Wolfe stated.

Breckenridge nodded. "Absolutely. It is not the reviews that concern me, nor is it the finances. The house has been full or very close to it for every performance, including the matinees, and we are about to extend the run. But . . . there is a tension that I cannot put my finger on and that is unlike anything I have ever seen. Members of the stage crew have felt it as well, I believe."

"As you can see, I am not suited to be an audience member in one of your theaters," Wolfe said, "so I am hardly qualified to speak about the Broadway stage and its vagaries. However,

I should think, given the artistic temperaments of the players, that tensions would be the rule rather than the exception."

"Yes, on that you are absolutely correct, Mr. Wolfe. It is rare, particularly in dramatic productions, when there is not some degree of strain among the cast members. Clashing egos, you know? But then, one does expect actors and actresses to have big egos—after all, it is part and parcel of who they are. Back to the tensions: In this case, they have been excessive from the beginning. Even during rehearsals, the backbiting and sniping were incessant, to the point where I began to wonder if I had erred in many of my casting choices. But I continued to believe everything would smooth out as we neared opening night."

"Does the producer normally select the players?" Wolfe asked.

"That is the case when I'm the producer," Breckenridge replied matter-of-factly. "I have always been extremely hands-on, particularly because I am the director as well."

"Perhaps you can be more specific about the individuals involved," Wolfe said. "Mr. Goodwin has seen the play, so he will know who is being discussed."

Breckenridge turned to me. "What did you think of it?"

"I thought it was very interesting," I answered, holding up the playbill as evidence of my attendance. "I was very surprised by the death near the end."

"You were supposed to be surprised," Breckenridge replied with a dry chuckle. "That is why, after the curtain falls and the applause dies down, one of the players—it's a different individual every performance—comes out and urges the audience members to keep the ending a secret from others who will be attending. The reviewers have been very good in this regard, too, suggesting to readers that the climax might very well come as something of a shock."

"Back to the individuals," Wolfe persisted.

"Yes, of course, sorry. I will start with Ashley Williston. She vigorously campaigned to get the role of Marjorie Mills, the grand dame of the once-wealthy family who is the focus of the play. Ashley has performed in dramas in New York and other American cities for twenty-five or thirty years and mistakenly fancies herself as the reincarnation of Helen Hayes or Gertrude Lawrence. She tends to be overly dramatic. As I have said, I function as director as well as producer, and my stage manager, who sees her as a real pain to work with, tried to talk me out of giving her the role."

"A role for which she hopes to finally get her Tony Award," I put in.

"Mr. Goodwin, it seems you know a good deal," Breckenridge said with a nod. "And yes, it is common knowledge around town that Ashley lusts after a Tony. At first, I was not enthusiastic about taking her on either, but I felt she effectively made a case for playing Marjorie. 'After all, Marjorie is something of a bitch, and so am I,' she told me. 'Think of it as typecasting, Roy.'"

Wolfe made a face. "Has Miss Williston proved difficult to work with?"

"About what I expected," Breckenridge said. "She tries to take over the directing at every opportunity, and we have had to rein her in a number of times. Then there's her animosity toward her costar, Brad Lester, who plays her feckless husband, Carlisle."

"Lester is a big name in Hollywood," I told Wolfe, "who is trying his hand at the stage."

"And doing a first-rate job of it," Breckenridge said. "That should be no surprise. After all, Brad has won one Oscar and been nominated for another. But most of his movie roles have been in action films, and it was my idea to cast him in this part because it is so different from what he's done on the screen, and I felt he had the versatility to handle the role. I was correct. Here he plays an absentminded, somewhat vague fellow in middle age who has never had to work very hard and doesn't have a real grasp of what's going on around him most of the time."

"What is the basis of Miss Williston's animus toward him?" Wolfe posed.

Breckenridge took a sip of the Bloody Mary and shifted in his chair. "Privately—well, not so privately, really—she refers to him as a 'Tinseltown pretty boy.' She claims to hold Hollywood and everything about it in low regard."

"Has she ever performed in motion pictures?"

"No, and were I to guess, she would jump at a plum movie role if it got offered, which is unlikely. There is one other thing fueling her anger: She believes I have put Brad in the cast for box-office appeal because her own star has dimmed."

Wolfe uncapped his second beer. "Is that true?"

Breckenridge favored us with a lopsided smile. "Yes, for the ears in this office only, although it has been a subject of a good deal of speculation around town and in the pages of *Variety*. Although, in Brad's defense, he is a lot more than a good-looking face. He has played the role very well and has gotten excellent reviews. In one of them, he was praised for 'making a most graceful shift from West Coast to East.'"

"What is his attitude toward Miss Williston?"

"Good question. On the surface, he behaves deferentially toward Ashley. She is somewhere between seven and ten years his elder—she guards her age—and of course she has long since earned her stripes on the stage, while he's a newcomer, so he is wise to be deferential, although this facade of his sometimes slips. Brad is polite to Ashley, but only superficially. After one performance, he was heard to say, sotto voce, 'I'd like to strangle that bitch.'"

"Who heard those words?" Wolfe asked.

Breckenridge colored slightly. "A stagehand. It always helps someone in my position to have eyes and ears everywhere in the theater, particularly backstage."

"Informers."

"A rose by any other name," the producer said. "But I do not apologize. There is a lot of money riding on the success of this show, as is the case with any Broadway production, for that matter."

"Surely there are more than two people in your cast," Wolfe said.

"Yes, indeed. Pardon me for the digressions. I have not been blessed with the gift of brevity. Steve Peters, who's a Broadway 'comer,' plays Larry Forrest, a wealthy nephew of Carlisle Mills who lost both of his parents in the crash of a private plane in the Caribbean, and as an only child, he is sole beneficiary of their millions. As the play opens, Larry is a house guest at Cresthaven. He has been invited by Carlisle and Marjorie— really by Marjorie—because she hopes he will share some of his wealth with them, which will enable them to hold on to the estate and keep it afloat. It's a huge old pile of stone and brick that is in desperate need of repairs."

"How has Mr. Peters fit into the cast?" Wolfe asked.

"Very well indeed. The man just turned twenty-eight, but he's a real pro, learns his lines quickly, is easy to work with, and takes direction well. He is also damned good-looking, which has not been lost on Ashley. She has always preferred younger men in her private life. She has been married twice but, currently, is unattached and doesn't like it. My sources"—Breckenridge grinned sheepishly at Wolfe—"tell me that she has been putting the make on young Mr. Peters, but he has shown no interest whatever in her, although he apparently has tried to rebuff her advances diplomatically. However, she seems not inclined to take no for an answer."

I know Wolfe well enough to realize he was disgusted with Ashley Williston's shenanigans, but he suppressed his revulsion. "Has this led to friction between them?" he asked.

Breckenridge nodded. "So I have been told and have also sensed. Apparently, Peters now goes to great lengths to avoid her backstage before and after the performances, although their dressing rooms are close to each other. For that matter, all the dressing rooms are cheek by jowl. The theater that we are in is not known for its amenities. But then, that is the case with most of these Broadway houses, many of which have been around for fifty or more years."

"Has this discord affected their performances?"

"Not in essence," the producer replied. "Whatever faults Ashley may have, she is a consummate professional once the curtain goes up. Neither I nor my stage manager has detected much tension between them—other than what is called for in the script, of course. After all, this is a drama that contains a lot of inherent tension. Let me correct myself," Breckenridge said. "There *have* been a couple of times when Ashley stepped on one of Brad's lines, and I'm sure it was intentional."

"For the record," I said to Wolfe, "I did not detect any false notes between Ashley and Peters when they were talking one-on-one onstage, which occurred several times. But then, when I saw the show, I wasn't looking for anything out of the ordinary, and I am hardly a critic."

Wolfe drained the last of his beer. "When contretemps occur between cast members, do you ever intercede?"

"Not if I can help it," Breckenridge said. "Although, as the producer as well as the director, I need to constantly be aware of personal situations. In the past, I have found it is best for players to work out problems of this sort without external interference. If I tried to inject myself into a situation like this, it might have an adverse effect on the performance of one or another of the principals. However, I must say that during rehearsals, I had to push back against Ashley when she made what I considered to be some niggling criticisms."

Wolfe leaned back, saying nothing. Breckenridge picked up the cue that it was time to move on.

"Another cast member is Melissa Cartwright, who plays Diana Gage, Larry Forrest's love interest in the story," he said. "Like Steve Peters, she is in her late twenties and, given her age, has had a good deal of Broadway experience, mostly as an ingénue, which is really the type of role she plays here. She's a redhead, wide-eyed and 'perky,' as one critic described her. She also is staying at Cresthaven because, when he got invited, Larry Forrest insisted that his fiancée also be included. This did not go over well with Marjorie for two reasons: First, she did not want outside interference when trying to persuade her nephew to loosen his purse strings. And second, she disapproved, at least outwardly, of an unmarried couple sharing a bedroom."

Wolfe turned to me, the signal that I was in the spotlight, and I knew what he wanted me to ask. "So, the youngsters, so to speak, are a couple onstage. Are they also a couple offstage?"

Breckenridge cut loose with a hearty laugh, which seemed somewhat forced. "I don't really think so, although I must say the idea did occur to me as well. One might-have-been affair between cast members is more than enough, thank you. As far as I know, both Steve and Melissa currently are unattached. He had a fling a while back with a leggy dancer in a hit musical that won several Tonys, but I think that dalliance ended amicably.

And I am afraid I do not have any clue as to Melissa's love life, although given her looks and personality, I would be surprised if she didn't have someone special. She is appealing, very appealing."

"Another cast member is that gabby old guy, the neighbor who drops in on the Millses all the time as if he considers himself part of the family," I said.

"Yes, that's Max Ennis, who plays Harley Barnes, a friend of the Millses. Max is a character actor who's been around for decades, one of those types who theatergoers instantly recognize but usually can't remember his name," Breckenridge said, turning from me to Wolfe. "His role is as a garrulous old family friend who is obsequious to the point of being a toady. He is obviously enamored of Marjorie, and he follows her around like a puppy with his tongue hanging out. So she has got a man she's tired of and another one she doesn't want. And as for poor Carlisle, he's oblivious to the whole scene. All he wants is to be left alone to play with his stamp collection and listen to his recordings from the Big Band era of the thirties and forties. Brad plays his part superbly. For that matter, so does Max."

"Is that all of the cast?" Wolfe asked.

"There's one more," Breckenridge replied. "Teresa Reed, who, like Max, specializes in character roles, in her case, acerbic middle-aged and outspoken crones who are indifferent to what others think of them. These roles of hers often provide a certain amount of comic relief, as is certainly the case in our production. Teresa plays Olive Hawkins, the combination maid and cook who is the last of a household staff that once numbered five, including a chauffeur. Throughout the play, she reminds her employers that 'things around here sure ain't what they once was.'"

"What is Miss Reed's personality away from the role?"

"Very much the same, sour and sarcastic. And it's *Mrs.* Reed," Breckenridge said. "In truth, she's pretty homely, tall and angular with a long face and a hawklike nose. But she does have a husband, Donald Reed, who is the house manager at another of the Broadway theaters."

Wolfe leaned back and considered the producer through narrowed eyes. "Based on what you have told me so far, sir, I fail to see the need for a private investigator. You stated there have been tensions and animosity among the cast but have supplied no particulars."

Breckenridge nodded ruefully. "You are right; let me get specific. I believe the trouble really stems from Ashley and her oversize ego, which impacts everyone around her and sets off a domino effect within the company. She clearly resents Brad Lester's presence, as I mentioned earlier, and her attitude toward Brad when they are not onstage has made him somewhat withdrawn. Then her transparent attempts to charm Steve Peters have caused him to be nervous and jumpy, and rather than lash back at her—he hasn't got the nerve for it, given her stature in the business—he tends to take out his frustration by snapping at Melissa Cartwright offstage. That upsets her, of course, and she sometimes withdraws into herself.

"One person in the cast who is not intimidated by Ashley is Teresa Reed, who, it is said, even chewed out the great John Gielgud once in London after a performance in which he had missed a cue. At least twice, Teresa has ripped into Ashley for her arrogance."

"How did Miss Williston respond to the attacks?" Wolfe asked.

"She backed down, although the net result was more tension among the cast. The only one who has largely avoided the backstage theatrics is Max Ennis, but even he has been heard to mutter that 'there's more damned electricity here than in a power plant. I just hope nobody gets fried by it.'"

Breckenridge finished his drink and shook his head when I made a move to get him a refill. "Now a certain amount of this behavior is to be expected in a play, particularly a drama. And the good news is that none of it seems to have spilled over into the performances to any degree—at least not yet. But I feel that something deeper is going on, although I can't articulate what it is. As I said before, I'm a hands-on guy, so I prowl the backstage areas a lot, and I sense the presence of evil. I know, I know, that sounds histrionic," he said. "You're probably thinking, 'this character has spent too much time in the thespian world,' which probably is true."

"I cannot conceive of ever using the word 'thespian,'" Wolfe said. "Continue."

"I don't know what else to tell you," the producer said, "other than to mention that whenever I'm walking around backstage, conversations suddenly stop, as if I've interrupted something that I am not meant to hear. I have never had that experience before."

"Do you feel personally threatened?" Wolfe asked.

He paused before answering. "I . . . I am not sure. But I do need help, and I have a proposal to put before you both."

# CHAPTER 4

Wolfe responded to Breckenridge's statement by buzzing for a third beer, one over his usual morning quota. He then turned to the producer, the signal for him to continue.

Breckenridge cleared his throat and readjusted himself. "Mr. Wolfe, I realize you do not venture out on cases, but Mr. Goodwin does, and I want to suggest an assignment for which I am prepared to pay your standard rates."

"I do not charge what you term 'standard rates.' Every commission is unique. What do you propose?"

"I need someone in the theater whom I can trust and who can spot trouble before it arises. And arise it shall; I am absolutely sure of this."

"You suggest Mr. Goodwin be a Caleb? Don't you already have people on your staff in that role?"

"A Caleb? I don't understand what you—oh, wait a minute. You are referencing the Bible, aren't you?"

"Caleb was a spy," Wolfe responded. "In the Old Testament book of Numbers, he is identified as the son of Jephunneh of the tribe of Judah and one of twelve spies sent by Moses into Canaan."

"I am most impressed, Mr. Wolfe," Breckenridge said. "I had no idea you were so devout."

"The Bible is literature, sir. One hardly need be devout to appreciate its intrinsic value."

"Of course. I do not see Mr. Goodwin taking precisely the role of a spy. My idea is that he would be a reporter for a Canadian theater magazine who has been sent to New York to interview the cast of *Death at Cresthaven* for a major feature in an upcoming issue. I would introduce him to everyone and ask that they make themselves available to him. I also would point out what good publicity this would be, especially given that thousands of Canadians are patrons of Broadway performances every year."

Wolfe exhaled loudly. "Am I to assume this publication would be fictional?"

"It would. We can give it any name we please," Breckenridge said. "It won't mean anything to our cast anyway. I happen to know that not one of them has ever appeared onstage in Canada."

Wolfe turned to me. "Archie, your thoughts?"

I did not like the idea. "What if someone recognizes me?"

"When did your photograph last appear in one of the New York newspapers?" Wolfe asked.

"It's been at least a couple of years."

"Mr. Breckenridge, we will discuss your idea and inform you of our decision."

The producer rose, realizing he had been dismissed. "When are you likely to make that decision?"

"We will not keep you waiting long," Wolfe said, also rising. "Good day."

I walked Breckenridge down the hall to the front door and helped him with his coat. "I could really use your aid here," he said, handing me his business card. "I hope you can persuade Mr. Wolfe to spare you for this project."

I did not respond, instead holding the door open. I watched the producer descend the steps to the street, hoping I could persuade Wolfe to *not* spare me for Breckenridge's crackpot project. I was ready to argue with him if necessary, but that would have to wait until we had finished our lunch of Fritz's superb sweetbreads amandine.

# CHAPTER 5

Back in the office with coffee after lunch, I figured I would wait Wolfe out. Let him bring up Breckenridge's proposal. But he decided to concentrate on the *New York Times* Sunday crossword puzzle, and for a half hour, not a word passed between us.

Finally, I gave up playing the silence game. "I thought for sure you would say something like 'preposterous' when the producer suggested I masquerade as a magazine writer. So since you have decided to go mute, I will say it: preposterous."

Wolfe set down the puzzle and his pen. "If you recall, you were the one who suggested we see Mr. Breckenridge and hear him out."

"I did, but that does not mean I have to like what I heard from him."

"I believe his proposal has some merit, Archie."

It was in that moment that I realized just how badly Wolfe wanted at least one of those *Grammangis spectabilis* orchids

Lewis Hewitt possessed. This sort of thing had happened before, so I should not have been surprised. "What we have here is a case of orchid lust, is that it?"

"I will not dignify that with a response."

"Heaven forbid you should. So you want me to become spy, a—what is it—a Caleb?"

"You and I can debate terminology later. Call Mr. Breckenridge and have him come here tonight; we will discuss how to proceed."

"So it's a done deal, eh? Okay, but he may not want to be away from the theater during a performance. After all, he has told us that he's the hands-on type."

"Very well," Wolfe snapped. "Make it eleven tomorrow morning."

I got hold of Breckenridge at his office, and he was delighted. "I'm so pleased Nero Wolfe is interested in pursuing this. I look forward to seeing you both tomorrow."

The next morning, our prospective client was right on time and beaming as I ushered him into the brownstone. "Last night's performance was our best one yet," he gushed. "Everyone was spot-on, and the audience responded with appreciation."

"I am glad to hear it," I said, steering him to the red leather chair in the office.

"Good day, sir," Wolfe said, asking our guest if he desired a drink, to which the response was a polite "No thanks."

"As you wish. Archie and I would like to hear more details of your plan. You have the floor."

"Thank you. Obviously, I do not want the cast, or anyone else involved in the production, for that matter, to feel that they are under surveillance."

"Although this is essentially what you are proposing," Wolfe said.

Breckenridge nodded. "Yes, it is, and I suggested Mr. Goodwin for the job because, through Lewis Hewitt, I am well aware of his tact and resourcefulness." I had all I could do to keep from throwing my telephone at him and his patronizing attitude.

"To review, you are suggesting Archie would appear at the theater as a magazine writer for a nonexistent Canadian publication specializing in theater, is that correct?"

"It is, and I would introduce him to the cast and the rest of the company, requesting their cooperation."

"What about photographs of those quoted in the article? Magazines like pictures. Who would take them?"

"I have already thought of that," Breckenridge said in a smug tone. "We possess an archive of dozens of excellent color photos of each of our principals, many of them taken during dress rehearsals. And we also have some shots taken during a performance."

"How long do you propose Archie continue this masquerade? If it goes on for more than a few days, members of your troupe will surely become suspicious. Magazines have deadlines, and they expect their writers to be efficient. Further, each member of your cast surely has been interviewed before, probably numerous times. They certainly have a good idea about how much time writers need."

"Your point is well taken," Breckenridge said. "I would expect this project to take two or maybe three days."

"What do you expect to gain from Archie's presence in the theater?"

The producer looked like he could use a drink after all, but I wasn't about to volunteer my bartending skills unless asked. "I would hope he could discover the source of the miasma that is infecting the company so I can deal with it," he answered. "That seems to be a reasonable expectation."

I felt as if I were watching a tennis match with me as the ball. And it seemed I had about as much say in the proceedings as the ball would.

"Archie would be given a different name, of course," Wolfe said. "And I assume you have created a title for this illusory magazine."

"Mr. Goodwin will be rechristened 'Alan MacGregor,' which is a good Scots-Canadian name, and the publication is to be called *StageArts Canada*, based in Toronto, which is a very fine theater city," Breckenridge said, looking pleased with himself.

"What do you think, Archie?" Wolfe asked.

"Mine is not to reason why. The sooner we get started with this deception, the better, as far as I'm concerned. I am ready to go at any time the two of you agree on."

"Before we go any further," Breckenridge said, "we need to discuss your fee, Mr. Wolfe. You will find me easy to deal with."

"It is very possible that after spending several days with the members of your company, Archie will not have come up with any information that will ease your concerns. I assume you understand that."

"I do. I am prepared to agree to any figure you dictate, and that figure is not contingent upon Mr. Goodwin's findings or lack thereof."

"Very well," Wolfe said. "Twenty thousand dollars now and another twenty thousand on completion of the assignment. Mr. Goodwin and I will be the sole judges as to when the assignment is concluded."

If Breckenridge was shocked, he did not show it. I can only assume Lewis Hewitt had prepared him for Wolfe's demands. The producer smoothly drew a checkbook and a gold fountain pen from the breast pocket of his suit coat and began to write.

"Would you like to telephone my bank?" he asked.

"No, sir," Wolfe replied.

"When can Mr. Goodwin begin?"

Wolfe turned to me. "I can start tomorrow," I said.

"Make it the day after," Breckenridge said, rising. "That will give me time to prepare everyone for your visit."

"So I am about to begin playing Caleb," I told Wolfe on my return to the office after seeing Breckenridge out. "Any instructions?"

"Only to use your intelligence guided by experience," he said, as he so often has. Before I could mount a snappy comeback, he had retreated behind his current book, *The Status Seekers* by Vance Packard. Rather than try talking to a wall, I got up and marched out to the kitchen to keep Fritz company as he prepared lunch.

# CHAPTER 6

Two mornings later, I donned a glen plaid sport coat, brown slacks, a tan shirt, and a brown-and-maroon–striped tie and considered the result in my bedroom mirror. I decided I could pass as a writer for a serious arts magazine from north of the border. After a breakfast of orange juice, scrambled eggs, Canadian bacon—which seemed fitting—and a blueberry muffin, I stood and saluted Fritz, announcing that I was "off to conquer the world of Broadway." His reply was a puzzled look, to which I said, "I will explain later."

I stepped out into a perfect August morning—bright sun, puffy clouds, and a tame breeze—so I decided to stroll the twelve blocks north to the theater district, where I was to meet Roy Breckenridge in a diner just west of Broadway.

The joint was long and narrow, with a counter and stools along the left side, most of them occupied, and at the back, two rows of booths with white Formica tabletops and red vinyl bench seats. Breckenridge occupied the rearmost booth on the left and hailed me with a sweep of the arm. "You are right on time, Mr. Goodwin," he said approvingly after checking his watch.

"Make it Archie," I told him. "I have never been big on formality."

"Excellent, nor have I. I go by Roy to almost everyone. Do you feel ready to go?"

"Yes, and since I spent a long weekend in Toronto a couple of years ago, I can even discuss that city to at least a small degree if asked. And I've even looked up the names of a couple of their legitimate theaters."

"I would not worry about that if I were you. Actors, and that includes many among this bunch you are about to meet, tend to be a self-centered lot, egotists who rarely ask questions of others and mainly want to talk about themselves and their careers."

"That will work out just fine, because asking questions is my forte. I assume they know I am coming today."

"They do. I told everyone about you yesterday and said that your magazine had chosen to write about *Death at Cresthaven* because of the excellent reviews it has received in the New York press. You will have no trouble getting them to talk, quite the contrary; you may have a hard time getting them to shut up."

"Do you have any suggestions as to the order in which I interview the cast and others?"

"You beat me to it with that question. For the purposes of keeping my most temperamental performer happy, I would appreciate it if you talked first to Ashley Williston. As you will soon learn from the horse's mouth, so to speak, she has convinced herself that she is carrying the burden of the whole show upon her slim and graceful shoulders. She will be happy to share with you the trials and tribulations of being absolutely indispensable."

"I can hardly wait to sit down with the woman," I said, grinning.

Breckenridge laughed. "I am glad to see your sense of humor is intact."

"It hasn't failed me yet, and a variety of individuals have put it to the test over the years."

"Including your employer, no doubt?"

"I make no comment, on the grounds that anything I say might tend to incriminate me."

That brought another laugh. "Have some coffee," he said, pouring a cup from a pot on the table. "The food here is only so-so, as you would expect, but the java is the best for blocks around, and I should know. Over the years, I've been in every hash house and beanery in the theater district." Breckenridge may have been right about the coffee's quality within the neighborhood, but the stuff wasn't nearly as good as what I had downed forty-five minutes earlier in the brownstone.

"I think of theater people as night types," I said. "And you have gathered them to see me at ten thirty in the morning. Should I expect a grumpy bunch?"

"Fortunately, we have a matinee today, so they've got to show up somewhat earlier than usual. Have you been backstage at a Broadway show before?"

"Surprisingly, only once, given the number of times I've been in the audience over the years. I met an actor after one of his performances, because he wanted to thank Mr. Wolfe and me for helping prove he did not commit a murder in which he had been a suspect."

"Hah! There are a few actors I wouldn't mind bumping off—no, just kidding," he said, holding up a hand. "Well, I will be gathering the cast and the stage manager this morning in the green room, where I'll introduce you. Then you can begin talking to them individually."

"Stage manager? Is he in charge of the action?"

Breckenridge snorted. "Sometimes this particular individual acts like he is the producer and director, which, last time I looked, were my titles. But in a way, he does run the show, at least in a day-to-day sense. He's an ornery sort, name of Hollis Sperry. Actually, I don't mind orneriness in my stage managers. They keep the cast from getting lazy and missing their cues, which a surprising number of actors are wont to do. He will chew out any actor if he deserves it, no matter how big a name he has."

"Sounds like a drill sergeant."

"That's a good analogy. When you have been verbally reamed out by Hollis, you won't forget it," Breckenridge said, glancing at his watch. "Let us head over to the palace where magic is created eight times a week."

We walked the two blocks to the Belgrave Theater, which, unlike a palace, presented a dingy, tired facade in daylight. When Lily and I had been there a few evenings earlier, the peeling paint on the walls and doors and the cracked sidewalk had not been readily apparent. We entered the building by the stage door in a gangway set back from the street and were greeted just inside by a rail-thin specimen with watery eyes who could have been anywhere from sixty to eighty.

"Morning, Mr. Breckenridge," the man said with a bow and a grin that showed gaps between nicotine-stained teeth. "Cast is all down in the green room like you asked, waiting for you. And Mr. Sperry, he's there too."

"Thank you, Connor," the producer said, introducing me and describing my role.

"A writer from Canada, eh?" the doorkeeper said. "I been to Canada myself once, Niagara Falls, it was, years back, but not on a honeymoon, no siree. Just there to see the sights." Connor started to go into detail about those sights, but Breckenridge tactfully cut him off, and we took a narrow iron stairway to the basement.

"Hardly glamorous down here, is it?" Breckenridge said. "But then, most people never see what goes on behind the scenes, which is a good thing, indeed, a very good thing. It would shatter the illusion we attempt to create, and we simply can't have that. I do everything I can to keep the public away from the backstage areas of my productions, particularly moonstruck stage-door Johnnies and autograph hunters. They can gather outside after a performance, but we won't let them in."

"Pay no attention to that man behind the curtain," I said.

"*The Wizard of Oz.* Oh, very good, very good!" Breckenridge said, clapping his hands. "That is my point precisely. We don't want our audiences to see that man behind the curtain. There is a certain magic to the theater, and we must do everything we can to sustain the magic. Here we are, the green room."

The first thing I noticed was that the room was not green, but gray, from the walls to the shabby carpeting and the sofa and chairs. The second thing was the faces of the assembled group: They ranged from indifferent to outright dour. Here was a group of individuals that clearly wished they were elsewhere, and I wondered if, as Breckenridge had said, they really would be eager to talk to me. I scanned those faces, identifying each cast member from the descriptions I had been given, along with the stage manager, who looked to be the least interested of them all.

"Thanks to each of you for coming this morning," Breckenridge said after clearing his throat. "It is my pleasure to introduce to you Alan MacGregor of the magazine *StageArts Canada.* He has come down from Toronto to do a feature on *Death at Cresthaven* for his publication.

"As most of you are aware, a great many Canadians patronize Broadway shows every year, and a goodly percentage of these folks read the magazine Mr. MacGregor works for. So please take the time to sit down with him and share your feelings and thoughts—all of them positive, of course—about our production." Breckenridge turned to me. "Anything that you want to add?"

"Just that I am happy to be here and anxious to spend time with each of you. I have seen the show, and I enjoyed it very much. I hope to pass along that excitement to our readers."

"Excellent!" Breckenridge said, nodding vigorously. "Because ours is a small cast, each member of the company has the luxury of his or her own dressing room, so I suggest these are where your interviews take place. Do you have a preference as to who you would like to start with, Mr. MacGregor?"

"If Miss Williston does not have any objections, perhaps I could talk with her first," I said, following Breckenridge's script.

"Objections? Not at all, none whatsoever," she replied airily. "Come with me to my palatial quarters, Mr. Toronto, and we shall palaver." She rose gracefully, gestured me to follow with a devil-may-care toss of a hand, and led the way as we departed from the not-at-all-green room.

# CHAPTER 7

"Very nice," I told Ashley Williston as we entered her dressing room, which had a sofa, a pair of wing chairs, two floor lamps, a multicolored three-panel Japanese screen behind which she could change, and the dressing table with the predictable vanity mirror surrounded by light bulbs.

"Mr. MacGregor, don't you know sarcasm when you hear it?" She sat, crossing one well-shaped leg over the other and watching me to see if that got a reaction as I took a seat opposite her. I held steady eye contact with the lady, however, and she went on. "You see before you the so-called 'luxury' that Roy Breckenridge described. I have had better dressing rooms than this in summer stock in one-horse towns upstate and in New England. Oh dear, I should not talk like that to a writer now, should I?" she said, placing a palm over her mouth in a gesture that was too cute by half. "After all, I am sure Roy wants each of us to tell you how we are just one big, happy family."

"Aren't you?"

"Oh, we really do get along quite well, better than a lot of casts that I have been a part of. Say, you look familiar to me; have we met somewhere before? I really am very good with faces."

"No, I'm sure I would have remembered it—maybe I have a twin; they say everybody does. In fact, when I got this assignment, I was pleased, because I would get to meet you."

"If you think flattery is going to get you anywhere with me . . . you are absolutely right. Have you seen me perform before?"

"Sadly, I had not, until a week ago. The biggest part of my job is writing about theater all across Canada, from Vancouver to Halifax and everywhere in between."

"You poor baby, I am afraid I don't envy you. Canada may be a big country, but it is mostly empty, isn't it?"

"Hey, you haven't lived until you've been to Moose Jaw and Medicine Hat," I told her, glad I had paged through the atlas back in the brownstone. I pulled a reporter's notebook and pencil from my pocket and took a moment to study Ashley. Although she had to be easily on the far side of fifty, she still was easy on the eyes, with her hair an ash-blond color and with good bone structure in her face. Close up, the makeup showed, but I knew from being in the audience that she cut quite a stunning figure on the stage. And she was aware of it.

"What was it that attracted you to the part of Marjorie Mills?" I asked, figuring that was a natural question for a reporter to open with.

"Where to start?" she said with a stagy flutter of manicured hands. "First off, I have always liked this playwright's work, and I've seen several of his creations, although I have never been in one before. Second, the role is just plain juicy; I play a grade-A bitch—maybe that's typecasting," she added with a self-deprecating laugh, perhaps hoping I would contradict her. "Third, I die dramatically, which I love, but you don't want to put that in your story, do you? It would ruin the suspense, which is a big part of the play's success. In a way, we are like that long-running Agatha Christie play, *The Mousetrap*, in that, after each performance, one of us urges the audience not to give away the ending to those who have not yet seen it."

"Yes, so I had noticed. You needn't worry; I will not ruin the surprise. Our publication is just as eager as you folks to avoid spoiling the experience for theatergoers. But I must say, your murder did come as a surprise to me."

"As it was indeed meant to," she said. "I believe most everyone thought Brad—who plays my husband, of course—would be the corpse, probably done away with by the Harley Barnes character in a fit of jealous rage. Max Ennis has played heavies often in the past, which probably is at least part of the reason Roy cast him."

"Do you enjoy working for Mr. Breckenridge?"

She paused a beat before answering, then nodded with a thoughtful expression. "Roy is . . . well, interesting to work for, to say the very least. We do not always see eye-to-eye, but that is to be expected when strong-willed people are involved, don't you think?" It was my turn to nod.

"There are a couple of things to be admired in Roy Breckenridge," she continued. "One, you always know exactly where you stand. And two, as both producer and director, he really takes total control of his production and monitors every aspect of it. Now that can also cause friction—in this case, particularly with the stage manager, Hollis Sperry. Of course you haven't talked to Hollis yet, have you?"

"You are the very first," I told her. "What am I likely to hear when I sit down with Mr. Sperry?"

"Oh dear, Mr. MacGregor, I probably said more than I should have." She did her palm-to-the-lips trick again, which was wearing thin. "I did not mean to foment trouble, not for a moment. Both men are very talented at what they do, and you may certainly quote me on that."

I scribbled dutifully in my notebook, although it was hardly necessary. I can recite long stretches of dialogue verbatim without a single notation, but I knew I had to act like a reporter.

"How about the other cast members? Would you say that you make a good team?"

"Well now, you have seen us in action, so I will turn that question around. What do you think?"

"I felt both the characterizations and the dialogue were very believable," I said, which was only a partial fib. "It seemed to me that you all meshed together extremely well."

She nodded and looked self-satisfied. "Good. I know that you must have seen God only knows how many shows in your line of work, so you are in a good position to judge." Now the flattery was flowing in the opposite direction.

"Talk for a bit about what you see as some of the strengths of the other cast members."

"Oh my, that is a wonderful question. Well, I will start with Brad Lester, my stage husband. Of course you know that he has made quite a name for himself in Hollywood, and that includes an Oscar—for a supporting role, that is. This has been his very first experience on the stage, and I feel that, all things considered, he has really done quite well, yes, quite well indeed."

"I'm sure you have been a great help to him, what with all of your experience. He must appreciate it."

"That is very kind of you to say, Mr. MacGregor. We do what we can with whatever talents we have been given."

"You mentioned Max Ennis earlier. I gather he has been around the theater for a long time."

"I'm surprised you hadn't heard of him. Yes, Max has been around as long as I can remember and then some. He's never had a leading role, but that doesn't mean he isn't talented. As I said, he often plays heavies—schemers, con artists, even killers on occasion. As you know from watching the show—and I hope you'll see us a few more times—Max plays a different type here, very obsequious and unctuous, what I would call a real toady."

"And very much enamored of the character you play," I put in.

"Yes, that's what the script calls for, and he plays it well, don't you think?"

"I do. Have you ever been in a production with him before?"

"Only once, which is surprising, given how long both of us have been around. I'm older than I look, Mr. MacGregor."

"I have no idea what your age is, and I am not about to ask."

That drew a dry laugh. "I'm glad of that, because I am not about to tell you. For the record, I had a birthday two weeks ago."

"A belated happy birthday."

"Thank you so much, Mr. MacGregor. I must tell you that I feel like I am in the prime of life."

"That's wonderful to hear. Any thoughts on the other members of the cast?"

"Mmm, well, Teresa Reed, who plays Olive, the combination maid and cook, is another Broadway fixture like Max who has been around seemingly forever."

"She comes off as a very caustic character."

"That is precisely the point, of course. Her cantankerousness—I believe that is the right word—adds some comic relief to a story line that is otherwise somber and angst filled. She has played that type many times, and I've never seen anybody who does it any better."

"Then we have the wide-eyed young couple who are lovebirds," I said. "In the show, they don't seem to realize what they've stumbled into—a cash-strapped household with a scheming woman, her oblivious husband, and a fawning neighbor who lusts after the lady of the house."

Ashley raised well-tended eyebrows. "Mr. MacGregor, I must say that you have very nicely summarized the situation at creaky old Cresthaven. And those 'lovebirds,' as you term them, are well portrayed by Steve Peters and Melissa Cartwright, both of whom are more experienced performers than one might gather from their youth and the naïveté they intentionally project on the stage."

"I did note from their biographies in the program that both of them have impressive résumés, which must have been a factor in why they got the parts."

"Oh yes . . . Roy Breckenridge is not one to take chances on totally untried performers. He is a very cautious man, which is well known around town and which has made it easier for him to attract backers for his shows. His instincts are trusted in the business."

"Both of the young cast members are quite attractive."

"Are they?" she responded with a blank expression. "Oh, I suppose that is true; I'm afraid I really hadn't noticed. Perhaps I am too involved in concentrating on my performance."

"A question about chemistry, Miss Williston. Once—"

"Ashley, please."

"A question about chemistry, Ashley. Once the parts had been cast, did all of you immediately hit it off, or was there a period of adjustment?"

She nodded. "That is a very insightful query, and one I have not been asked before. In all candor, I don't believe I have ever been part of a production in which all its players immediately bonded with one another. Perhaps it is our vanity, our egos. We tend to approach those with whom we are going to perform cautiously, warily. And not one of the six of us in *Cresthaven* had ever been in a cast with any of the others before—oh, except those times years ago that I mentioned when Max Ennis and I were in the same play, but we were never onstage together in that instance."

"Does that unfamiliarity with one another indicate that things were rocky at the start?" I asked.

"Oh, I did not mean to suggest that, not at all," she said. "It's just that it took time during rehearsals for everyone to find their . . . I guess *rhythm* is the word. Yes, that's it, rhythm."

"No jealousies?"

A pause. "Not that I am aware of, but actors can be very good about hiding their feelings, so you might want to ask that of the others."

"How do the others feel about working for Mr. Breckenridge?"

She smiled tightly. "Once again, you will have to ask them that question. As I said a moment ago, Roy is all right, a bit too controlling sometimes perhaps, but please don't quote me on that."

"I won't. Any other observations you'd like to make about the show, the reviews, the audience reaction, or any of your fellow cast members?"

"I don't think so," she said. "You can say this has been an exhilarating experience for me, and that several people who have seen the show have approached me in restaurants and on the street telling me how much they had enjoyed seeing it. That is so very heartening, Mr. MacGregor. As long as I have been in the business, I never tire of hearing that."

"Thank you so much for your time," I told her, rising. "I may want to talk to you again."

"It would indeed be my pleasure," she said with a practiced and insincere smile, holding out an outstretched arm as she remained seated. The way she presented the slender and well-tended hand to me, it seemed that she expected me to kiss it. I shook it gently instead. It would not be proper for a writer to get too personal with one of the subjects of his article, not that I was inclined in that direction with Ashley Williston.

# CHAPTER 8

I stepped out of Ashley's dressing room and closed the door gently behind me, almost colliding in the narrow hallway with Steve Peters, the youthful actor playing Larry Forrest, wealthy nephew of Carlisle and the man the Mills family hoped would be their financial savior.

"Oh! I'm sorry, Mr. MacGregor," he said, giving me a sheepish smile. "I have a bad habit of looking down when I'm walking and thinking at the same time."

"If that is the worst habit you have, consider yourself fortunate. I am not going to tell you what some of mine are. Do you have time to talk for a little while?"

"Yes, sir. Yes, I do—if you don't mind meeting in my dressing room. I hope you are not claustrophobic."

"Nope, I was once stuck between floors on a crowded elevator for fifty minutes, and I never flinched. I'm sure your quarters will seem spacious by comparison."

"Do not be too sure of that," Peters said, opening his door. Okay, so his dressing room wasn't spacious—about half the size of Ashley Williston's—and it had only one chair, which the actor insisted I take.

"Can I pour you some ice water?" he said, motioning to a carafe on a small table. "I'm afraid it's all I've got."

I declined politely, wondering why the oh-so-elegant Miss Williston had not offered me anything to drink, given her exalted status.

"Glad you can work me in," I told the dark-haired young actor as I pulled out my notebook.

"No, I am glad you can work *me* in," he countered. "After all, I am just a small cog in this operation."

"You don't seem like a small cog, in any sense, when you're out on the stage," I said. Peters was one good-looking guy, no question, with a strong chin, full head of well-groomed dark hair, and blue eyes. But he also seemed right at home in his role, and I told him so.

"Well, thank you," he said earnestly, leaning forward and resting both elbows on his knees. "I probably should not be telling a reporter this, but I was nervous at first during rehearsals, being on the same stage with Ashley Williston and Brad Lester and the others. Now, though, I am a lot more relaxed."

"To what do you attribute that?"

He turned his palms up. "Partly getting to know the others, partly some encouragement I got."

"From whom?"

"I guess you could say Ashley Williston took me under her wing," he said, his face coloring slightly. "From the start, she has been very encouraging."

"I'm pleased. I realize actors and actresses are known for their artistic temperaments, although perhaps some of that is a fiction. Has there been much tension among all of you, either during rehearsals or during the run itself, for that matter?"

I could tell Peters was becoming nervous with this line of questioning and I felt sorry for him, but I pushed on. "I suppose a certain amount of tension is to be expected in any play, particularly a drama."

"Well . . . I have taken some good-natured razzing," he said. "I'm a graduate of the Yale School of Drama, and the other cast members, especially the older ones, like to refer to me as 'Our resident Yalie.' They all like to say they graduated from 'the school of hard knocks.' Sometimes, when I get to the theater, they all start singing 'Boola Boola.'" When I looked puzzled, he quickly added, "It's an old Yale fight song."

"Do the others also rib Miss Cartwright? She is about your age, isn't she?"

"She's just a little older, a year or so, I think, but she attended a state school, and she likes to refer to me as a Yalie, too." I got the impression from Peters's tone that maybe not all the razzing was that good-natured.

"It's not like you are new to the business," I said. "I have read your bio, so I know you've appeared in several Broadway productions."

"'True, and overall, I have received good reviews, although my parts were minor. I don't want to appear overly sensitive, Mr. MacGregor. I get along just fine with everybody in the production—cast, stagehands, lighting crew, box-office staff, stage manager . . .'"

"So you have assimilated. And I assume you also have a good relationship with Roy Breckenridge."

"Yes, I do. In fact, Mr. Breckenridge is the one who suggested me for a role in the production. He had seen me last year in *Autumn of a Tycoon* and asked that I read for the role of Larry

Forrest, the rich nephew who the Millses hope will be their financial salvation, and—well, I don't need to tell you this; you have already seen the show."

"And enjoyed it. You sound like you take the teasing you've gotten with good humor."

Peters hunched his shoulders. He had seemed much more self-possessed on the stage than he did here with me, one-on-one, so I switched to a safer subject. "Do you have any thoughts about the types of roles you would like to take on after this production is done?"

"I'm open to just about anything," he said. "I have a new agent, and he seems quite well connected, so there could be all sorts of possibilities. I like to think I'm optimistic by nature."

"Back to *Death at Cresthaven*. Do you have any other comments about the production? Anything at all that might be interesting to our readers up there in the friendly country just to the north?"

"I think that if they come down to New York to see us, which I hope they do, they will enjoy a top-notch show with a first-rate cast." He laughed. "Hey, I sound like a press agent, don't I?"

"There's nothing wrong with that. A good artist should take pride in his work and promote it."

"I guess I'm an artist of sorts," he said, laughing again in a self-deprecating way. "I hope others think so." I was left to wonder if the "others" he referred to were theatergoers or his fellow cast members.

I realized I wasn't going to wring anything more out of young Mr. Peters, at least not now. "I've taken enough of your time," I told him as I rose. "I hope the matinee performance goes well."

"For some reason, don't ask me why, I always seem more relaxed before the matinees," Peters said. "It must have something to do with my metabolism, do you think?"

"You are asking the wrong guy about that," I said. "I've never understood what metabolism is or how it works. Is it still okay for me to tell you to break a leg today, or has that become a cliché on Broadway?"

"No, it's still done, and I think it always will be," he said. "Thank you for talking to me."

"It is I who should thank you," I replied as I stepped out into the hall.

# CHAPTER 9

I checked the time, figuring I could work in one more interview before the cast had to get ready for the matinee. Walking a few paces along the dingy hall, I stopped at a door with TERESA REED printed on a card set into a slot that probably had held the names of countless actors and actresses over the years. I knocked once.

"Yes?"

"Mrs. Reed, it is Alan MacGregor. Would you be able to talk to me for a few minutes?"

The door swung open, and I found myself facing a tall and scowling sixtyish woman with a long face dominated by a chiseled nose and eyes that probably were dark brown but looked black to me. "Well, come on in," she said with a nasal sigh. "I knew I would have to see you eventually, so it might as well be now."

Her room was smaller than Ashley Williston's but bigger

than Peters's, probably signifying the pecking order within the cast. She stepped aside and said in a sour tone, "Welcome to my home. Can I get you something to drink? I have Coke, coffee, and a wretched red wine that someone—I can't remember who—gave me as a 'gift of appreciation' for my performance." Teresa behaved exactly as she did in the play: caustic and acerbic. Maybe she was always in character.

"Nothing for me, thanks," I said as I settled into a wing chair she had indicated with a nod. She parked herself on a sofa.

"So what do you want to know?" she said, crossing her arms over her chest.

I gave her what I hoped was a winning grin. "What in particular is there about this show that attracted you?"

"The money," she said with a dry laugh that carried no mirth. "Seriously, the part is one I knew I could play well. You've covered the theater world long enough, I assume, to have seen me before. You can see that I'm ideally suited for the role of Olive Hawkins, cranky, wisecracking. It's what I have been doing for years."

"And have always done very well," I said. "I—"

"You don't sound like a Canadian," she interrupted.

"I'm not, at least not originally. I come from Ohio," I said, having anticipated the question and glad I could be honest about something.

"Where in Ohio?" she demanded.

"Chillicothe," I said, the honesty now oozing from every pore.

She nodded, unsmiling. I wondered if she ever smiled. "The reason I asked is that I lived in Toledo when I was a kid about a thousand years ago. Have you ever been there?"

"No, never."

"Well, you haven't missed a blessed thing," she said, torching a cigarette with a match before I could pull my lighter out. "I have never been back, and I've never had any urge to."

"I haven't been back to Chillicothe, either, except for very occasional visits. Do you find the chemistry good in this production?"

She raised razor-thin shoulders and let them drop. "It's all right, I guess. I'm not big on what you call *chemistry*," she said, exhaling smoke. "I play my part, and I expect everyone else to do so as well. That's called professionalism where I come from. No temperament, no fuss, no histrionics. To hell with all of that. If it's anything I cannot stand, it is prima donnas of both sexes who take themselves too seriously and think that method acting is the only way to go."

"Are you suggesting there are prima donnas in *Death at Cresthaven*?"

"Don't try to put words in my mouth for the purpose of spicing up your story, young man," she rasped, gesturing with a bony hand. "I am merely telling you that I can't abide pretentiousness in this business. Do not try to foment dissent at my expense."

"I would not think of it, Mrs. Reed. One of the goals of our publication is to make the theater appealing to our readers."

"I suppose that's a noble goal," she conceded with a snort. "What else can I tell you?"

"What's it like working for Roy Breckenridge?"

She ground out her barely smoked cigarette in a metal ashtray and pulled another one from a pack. This time I was ready with my Zippo. "Breckenridge? He's all business, has to be to keep the backers happy. I don't very often work for somebody who's both the producer and director, and that takes some getting used to."

"How so?"

"He's awfully hands-on, involved in every aspect of the production. He might just as well be the stage manager, too. He watches almost every performance from his cubbyhole."

"Oh? What's that?"

She let loose with another joyless chuckle. "There's a booth at one side of the stage that is soundproofed and has a window that looks out on the stage. And it's wired for sound. Most nights, Breckenridge hunkers down in there drinking gallons of Coca-Cola and monitors what goes on. He takes pages of notes then goes over them with Hollis; that's Hollis Sperry, the stage manager. Have you met him?"

"Not yet. I just saw him in the green room earlier."

"Huh! So you have got that treat to look forward to. Anyway, Hollis gets all these notes from on high, so to speak, and then he goes over them with us." It was clear from Teresa Reed's tone that she was less than pleased with the procedure.

"I should know the answer given how long I've covered theater, but are cubbyholes like this common in Broadway houses?"

"That is a very good question," she said. "As far as I know, this theater is the only one that's set up that way, and who installed it, I have no idea, but it's been there for years.

"And that is at least part of the reason why most if not all of Breckenridge's productions are staged in this house. He didn't have the cubbyhole built, but when he learned about its existence, he fell in love with the thing and he's been using it ever since."

"It sounds like he's a perfectionist."

"Oh yes, and then some." She sniffed. "But I knew that going in; after all, I've worked for the man before, and chances are I will work for him again."

"Have any of the other cast members been in Breckenridge productions before?"

"Mmm, I'll have to think about it. Of course, Peters and

Cartwright are relative newcomers, so they're probably in one of his shows for the first time. Let's see . . . That leaves Ashley, Lester, and Max. You can scratch Lester, since he hasn't been on Broadway before. As for Her Highness—don't quote me," she said with a conspiratorial grin. "I am not positive that she ever worked for Roy, although she might well have. But now Max is another story. He has been in so many shows that I've lost count. I've never worked with him before, although I've known him for ages and I like him. We're a pretty small community, when you come down to it. At one time or another, he has probably toiled under every impresario in this town and has likely been on every stage in this town as well, both on and off Broadway. Have you spoken to him yet?"

"No, I'll try to see him after the matinee."

"Well, then, you can ask him yourself. After all, you are a reporter, aren't you?"

I had to concede the lady was correct, and I excused myself, figuring I would track down Breckenridge, assuming that he could spare a few minutes for me as we approached curtain time.

# CHAPTER 10

I had no trouble locating the producer. He stood on the darkened set talking to a couple of stagehands. I stood a respectful distance away until he noticed me. "Ah, Mr. MacGregor, did you want to see me?"

"Whenever you have a moment, no hurry."

He said something to the stagehands, and they walked away, nodding. "How have your interviews gone?" he asked in a voice just above a whisper.

"I talked to three of your cast members, and I plan to talk to the rest of them as well as the stage manager after the matinee, then I'll give you a rundown. But first, I just learned about your so-called 'cubbyhole.'"

He laughed. "I guess I had not mentioned it to you, had I? It just slipped my mind because it's become such an integral part of my operations. Come on, I'll show it to you." We walked off the stage and into the wings, where Breckenridge indicated a door, pulling it open and gesturing me to go inside.

The cubbyhole was about four times the size of a front hall closet and had a glassed window in one wall that looked out on the stage. A tall padded chair was situated behind a control panel that had a couple of buttons and a microphone.

"This is soundproofed," he said, "and it is blended into the set in such a way that it is camouflaged from the audience. I'm in here for almost every show drinking Cokes, and by turning this dial, I can clearly hear every word spoken on the stage. I sometimes use this during rehearsals when I'm not out on the stage or sitting down front, and I take notes during the performances. I know the cast and crew think I'm obsessive, but that is the way I operate and always have."

"So you had this little room built?" I asked.

"No, no, that was done years ago by someone else, I don't even know who. Maybe someone who was as compulsive as I am. But when I learned of its existence, I decided I would try to stage all my productions in this house, assuming it was available."

"And has it been?"

"Almost without exception. This is my seventh production here," he said. "I don't think I could operate without my little room now. Afraid I've become spoiled."

"And why not? If something works, stay with it."

"I could not have said it better myself. I trust you will stay and watch the matinee from the wings. And catch tonight's performance as well."

"I will. Are you still feeling uneasy in general about the show?"

"Yes, I am. I still can't precisely tell you what's eating at me, but that is where I'm hoping you are going to help. They're about to open the doors," he said, glancing at his watch, "so the audience will begin filing in. Looks like we'll have a full house or close to it; we're getting three big groups today that are being bused in from Westchester County."

I spent most of the next forty-five minutes avoiding the bustling stagehands and other functionaries, as well as Hollis Sperry, the dyspeptic stage manager, who carried a clipboard and barked orders while grumbling about how nobody ever listened to him. He grumbled about me, too, and suggested a place for me to stand—an alcove on stage left, which is really on the right side of the stage as viewed from the audience. I was learning the lingo.

Even though this was my second time experiencing *Death at Cresthaven*, the view from the wings made it seem like I was watching an altogether different production. I quickly learned why Sperry had positioned me where he did: all the cast members made their entrances and exits from stage right, so I was never in their way.

The whole of the three-act play was set in one room, the dark and somewhat threadbare Victorian parlor of Cresthaven, circa 1940. As the curtain rose, Ashley Williston, as Marjorie Mills, clad in an elegant peach-colored dress, entered to applause.

When the clapping subsided, she addressed her husband, Carlisle, played by Brad Lester, as he sat on an overstuffed davenport reading the *New York Times*.

"Darling, you do remember that Larry is arriving today, with that *friend* of his, don't you?"

He looked up at her over half-glasses that added to his age. "Hmm. Oh yes, yes . . . of course. Coming up on the train from the city, I believe, isn't he?"

"You know very well that he is, Carlisle. I've said so to you enough times. I have asked Harley to pick them up at the three-ten. Lord, it's been what . . . four years since we've seen Larry, or maybe longer. Do you remember when he came through that time before taking off for Europe? Of course, that was before the terrible crash of that small plane in Aruba, killing his dear, dear parents, Charlie and Grace. We haven't laid eyes on the boy since they've been gone, other than at the dreary double funeral in that dreary Philadelphia suburb."

"No, no we haven't," Carlisle said as he continued to focus on whatever it was that interested him in the *Times*.

"Of course he is hardly a boy anymore," Marjorie went on. "He must be close to thirty now, don't you think?"

"Mmm."

"Honestly, Carlisle, I don't believe that you have heard a word I've been saying."

"But I have, my dear," he said softly, looking up at her and blinking. "Something about that dreary Pennsylvania funeral and how Larry really isn't a boy anymore."

"All right, so you were listening, at least with one ear, which is more than I can usually hope for. I'm having Olive prepare lamb chops for dinner. Do you think that's all right? She is usually good with lamb chops."

"Usually . . . I think," Carlisle answers with brows knitted, drawing laughter from the audience.

"Well, she's all we've got in the way of a staff these days, as you well know."

"But you are hoping that my nephew is going to come to our rescue, aren't you, my dear?" Carlisle said in a gentle tone, setting the paper down and rising.

"After all, he is now a multimillionaire with no siblings, no children, and no other relatives closer than you," she said. "Is it too much to expect for him to share some of your late younger brother's estate with us? You told me that when you and Charlie were young, you looked after him and helped him with his homework and protected him from bullies. As it turned out, he went off to Princeton and ended up making a fortune with that big drug company in New Jersey while you . . ." She stopped herself and adjusted a figurine on an end table.

"While I went to a state university and ended up in middle management with an insurance company before my heart attack and that minuscule pension I received," Carlisle said, finishing his wife's sentence. "I know people said I married you for your money, but . . ."

"Now I did not mean to suggest—"

"And then, of course, our money—well, *your* money, really— ran out, partly because of some unwise investments on my part, and so here we are today, my dear, the genteel poor."

"Do not say that!" she snapped. "We are *not* poor."

Carlisle responded with a tired smile and walked out. "I will be in the study," he said over his shoulder.

"I know, playing with your stamp collection," she replied with an edge to her voice, although she had lost her audience of one. Olive Hawkins entered, coughing once and announcing that she was "preparing the lamb chops along with mashed potatoes and spinach, and for—"

"You know very well that I abhor spinach," Marjorie huffed.

"I also know very well that it is good for you, better than most of the things you insist on eating," the cook-cum-maid shot back in a tone that suggested no further discussion. "Things around here sure ain't what they once was," she said to a smattering of applause. She would mouth the line several more times in the play, and if the audience reaction was similar to what I had seen earlier, that applause would grow with each repetition.

And Olive wasn't through yet. "As I started to say before I was interrupted, for dessert I will be serving strawberry ice cream." Not waiting for a reply, she executed a snappy about-face and marched out, head held high. More applause.

"If we didn't need that woman right now, so help me, I would . . ." Marjorie sighed and threw herself into a high-backed chair, picking up a magazine and paging through it idly. The doorbell rang.

"Olive, the door!" the lady of the house keened after the third ring. Finally, with another protracted sigh, she left the parlor through French doors. When she returned, three others were trailing behind her.

"Train was right on time for a change," said a portly, florid-faced man, next-door neighbor Harley Barnes, played by Max Ennis. "I knew who they were right away, of course."

"Larry, it is so, so wonderful to see you," Marjorie effused, offering her husband's nephew her hand.

"Aunt Marjorie, I want you to meet my fiancée, Diana Gage," he said, stepping back gracefully as the two women shook hands.

"Thank you so much for your hospitality," Diana said with an engaging smile. "I am so glad to meet you at last. I have heard so much about you."

"I have heard so much about you, too, my dear," Marjorie said. "We simply *must* get to know each other. Now, you both must be exhausted from the ride on that dirty old New Haven line train. Why they don't clean up their cars, I will never know. It is a disgrace, an absolute disgrace. I will show you up to your rooms, and you can freshen up before dinner."

"And I will carry their luggage upstairs," Barnes said, ever the helpful sycophant. The young couple, played by Steve Peters and Melissa Cartwright, looked older when viewed from the wings than from the audience, maybe because their makeup was more apparent up close.

Now that all the cast have made an appearance, I will not subject you to more of the play, except to say that Marjorie Mills is found dead on the terrace in Act Three, strangled with her own silk scarf. The culprit, eventually identified by Larry Forrest, was Harley Barnes, who had long carried a torch for the woman. He was overheard (by Forrest) professing his undying love for her, and she laughed at him.

The audience sees only a shadowy figure attempting to embrace a spot-lit Marjorie on the terrace, and when she resists, she is strangled, writhing dramatically before her demise. Before the denouement, audience members, or so it was hoped by the playwright, suspected either her husband or Larry Forrest himself, with whom she had been flirting. I have no qualms about revealing the ending, as the play closed suddenly after a brief, but healthy and profitable, run, and to my knowledge, it has not yet been restaged anywhere.

# CHAPTER 11

The audience, which gave what seemed to me to be enthusiastic applause, filed out of the theater after three curtain calls. I went to Breckenridge's cubbyhole, knocking once and entering. "Would you rank that as a good performance?" I asked, poking my head in.

He swiveled in his chair and nodded. "Yes, I would say so," he replied, finishing the last of a glass of Coca-Cola. "One or two pauses were a beat too long, but otherwise, a competent job. I would give it a B-plus. Everybody was where they should be, when they should be, as I would expect. I scribbled comments on just a few minor things, which is good. I'll have to see what Hollis thinks. We always compare notes after a performance."

"Well, the folks who paid the freight seemed to like it, if that's any sort of a measuring stick."

"The matinee crowds are usually the easiest to please," he said. "Maybe that's why I love them so much."

"I'll want to talk to the rest of the cast and Sperry this afternoon. Do you see that as a problem?"

"Not at all. On days when we have two performances, it's good that they have something to occupy them during the in-between time. Feel free to start with anyone you like."

"I think I'll begin with your stage manager, unless you want to see him first."

"No, that's just fine. We've got hours before the curtain goes up again."


I found Hollis Sperry at his small desk at stage right, from where he watched every performance with his notebook at the ready. I wondered if he envied Breckenridge's more comfortable vantage point.

"Pardon me, Mr. Sperry. If possible, I'd like to grab a few minutes of your time now."

"Huh! Oh yeah, yeah, it's MacGregor, isn't it?" he said, seeming distracted. "Hell, I guess now's as good a time as any. How 'bout the green room? I could use a fresh cup of coffee."

He got his coffee from a pot on a side table and we settled into two stuffed chairs. Hollis Sperry was at least sixty with gray hair slicked back and the build of a jockey. He wore an open-collared, striped shirt and dark pants held up by suspenders. His narrow face seemed to be frozen into a permanent scowl.

"I hear you've been around for a long time. You must have seen a lot of fine theater over the years."

"Yes, sir, that is all too true. I've watched a lot of the greats, all right, and a goodly number of the not-so-greats as well—unfortunately, many more of the latter."

"And you've probably seen all kinds of personalities as well."

"I have that. Everyone from egomaniacs, and there are

plenty of them, to a handful of performers who are basically so shy and withdrawn that you wonder how and why they ever got into the theater, or even wanted to. These types pose a real challenge to the director, but the payoff can be very rewarding, both to us behind the scenes and to the audiences. There are a few big names on Broadway—I won't get specific—who used to totally freeze up during rehearsals."

"Back to *Death at Cresthaven*. Were you pleased with this afternoon's performance?"

He shrugged. "Not bad, not bad. We have gotten better every day. The run started out a little rough from my point of view, but that's not unusual, especially when you've got a bunch who haven't worked together before."

"Do they all get along with one another?"

He paused, drinking coffee. "More or less. Hell, I really don't care how well actors like each other as long as they know their lines; enter, stand, or sit where they're supposed to; and stay in character, for God's sake. This bunch seems to be doing that pretty well on the whole. But there is always room for improvement."

"Any area in particular where you would like to see improvement?"

Taking another sip of coffee, Sperry clearly was uncomfortable being interviewed. "Nothing special I can single out. Maybe cut down on some of the pauses in the dialogue. By that, I mean they need to be a half second quicker in responding to what someone else says. We've talked about that, and I have seen things get better."

"But as you just said, there's always room for improvement."

"Yeah, one thing you've really got to guard against is complacency, which is so doggone easy to fall into. I was stage-managing another play a while back—I'm not going to mention it by name—which got great reviews, raves," he said. "And it had a heck of a cast of old pros, well-known names in the theater world. But after a few weeks, they started getting sloppy and careless. The director—you would recognize his name, since you know a lot about this business—he was too easygoing, and I had one devil of a time trying to keep everybody in line. Problem was, they all knew that the reviewers wouldn't be back for a second look unless there were major changes in the cast. I must have aged ten years in that job."

"Do you think something like that could happen here?"

"There's always a chance, of course, but Roy Breckenridge is on top of everything as the director and also the producer—and a major investor, too, for that matter. If this show were to flop, he would end up being a big loser where it really hurts—in the pocketbook—and I do not believe that is about to happen. He won't let things slide any more than I will. We are in agreement in that regard."

"So the two of you get along well?"

For the first time, the stage manager allowed himself the hint of a smile. "Well . . . I didn't exactly say that, did I? We are both strong-minded, and we occasionally disagree on one thing or another. But overall, I do like the way Roy runs the show. He doesn't put up with carelessness or a lack of professionalism any more than I do. He's one of the few directors I respect."

"This production figures to have a long run, doesn't it?"

Sperry nodded. "Looks that way, all right, although I am a pessimist by nature. I don't ever take anything for granted. If something can go wrong, it will. We could have an earthquake tomorrow."

"In New York? I doubt it. Anything else you'd like to add? Any question I should have asked?"

"Seems like we've covered things pretty well. Do you figure articles in that Toronto magazine of yours will result in people actually coming down here to get rid of some of their hard-earned Canadian dollars?"

"I like to think so, yes. Toronto is a good theater town, and people up there pay a lot of attention to what's going on in New York."

"Ah, there's nothing to compare with the glitter and swank of Broadway, the Great White Way."

"Can I quote you?"

That brought a full-fledged laugh from the taciturn Sperry. "Darn right you can quote me. You got the spelling of my name?"

I said I did and thanked him for his time, then set off in search of my next victim.

# CHAPTER 12

Chance dictated that my so-called victim was a very attractive one: Melissa Cartwright, who had just stepped out of her dressing room as I walked down the hallway from the green room.

"Hi, Mr. MacGregor," she said brightly, then stuck out her lower lip in a pretend pout. "I feel slighted that you haven't talked to me yet."

"Put your mind to rest," I told her. "The time is now. Where should we rendezvous?"

"Definitely *not* in that horrible green room or in my dumpy dressing room," she said with feeling. "I spend enough time in those places as it is. On days when we have two performances, I like to get out of the theater for a while. There's a little spot over on Ninth Avenue that makes a marvelous bowl of chili. Can I tempt you?"

"Tempt away and lead the way," I said, playing the role of a visitor to the city. I did not take long during our two-block stroll to learn that the young lady was a chatterbox, which I attributed in part to nervous energy. I noticed as we walked west that she looked younger and more fetching without makeup, and that her turned-up nose seemed more pronounced than it did on the stage.

"I don't know any Canadians," she said. "How would you describe yourselves as a people?"

"I am really not the right person to answer that." I laughed, telling her about my Ohio roots. "But I say to you that most of the people I've met in my years in Toronto are friendly, although, in general, more quiet and reserved than Americans, particularly Midwesterners like me."

"I call myself a Midwesterner, too," she said, "from Lansing, Michigan. Have you heard of it?"

"Yes, but that's about all. What can you tell me about Lansing?"

"Well, for one thing, it's the state capital," she said. "Plus, it is the city where they make all those Oldsmobiles. My father works for Olds; he's an executive in the marketing department. And, oh yes, we have Michigan State right there in the neighborhood, too, the first land grant college in the country. That's where I went to school," she said with a touch of pride.

"So that makes you a Spartan, doesn't it?" I said, thereby exhausting my sports-page knowledge of the place.

"Yes, it does," she said. "Three cheers for the green and white! You could call me a 'townie,' I suppose, for going to school in my hometown, although I always lived on the campus. Here is the place I was talking about, Mr. MacGregor."

I had passed this beanery before but had barely noticed it and never stopped in. It didn't look like much from the street, and the interior was far from special, although the aroma made up for the decor. Chili has never been on the brownstone's menu, but I happen to like it, so I was happy to learn it was the specialty in this outwardly unimpressive joint.

"So nice to see you again," a smiling, hennaed hostess said to Melissa. "You just can't resist our chili, can you, hon?"

"By now, you know me too well," the actress said, grinning back. "And look, I've even brought along a friend. Do I get extra credit for that?"

"How about we give you booth number one as a reward?" She gestured toward a table in the front window.

"Is this okay with you?" Melissa asked.

"Absolutely," I said. "I have never in my life been one to turn down the best seat in the house."

"Now, isn't this better than us talking back there in that cramped theater?"

"It is without doubt," I answered. "And just to get things straight from the start, this is my treat."

"Oh, no, I did not expect you to buy my lunch, Mr. MacGregor. I am planning to pay."

"As a journalist, I simply cannot take a free meal," I said with a smile. "That would compromise my objectivity when talking to one of the subjects of an article."

"Well, if you put it that way, I guess I accept," she said, tilting her head in a practiced gesture. Practiced or not, I liked it.

After we had ordered our bowls of chili, I pulled out my notebook. "Tell me a little about your background."

"As I mentioned, I went to Michigan State and was in the theater department. I acted in several student productions and got good reviews from the local daily paper and the campus paper and also from my professors. While still in college, I did summer stock up in New England, and I got some nice notices there as well."

"Sounds like you got hooked on the theater business early."

She nodded, showing dimples. "For sure, and after graduation, I came straight to New York, like so many other starstruck hopefuls, all full of optimism and excitement. I was absolutely positive I would land some big part quickly."

"And you did?"

"And I didn't," she said, shaking her head as our chili arrived. "Oh, I got a few crumbs, small roles, mostly off-Broadway, and I was in the chorus line at a musical that closed after three weeks. That abrupt ending didn't bother me much, though, as I really prefer dramas to musicals, and I only took that chorus line job so I could keep eating."

I laughed. "I like your candor. I read in the playbill that you had been in a number of New York productions before *Cresthaven*."

"Yes, I started getting noticed after a couple of those off-Broadway shows," she said as we began attacking the chili. It lived up to the advanced billing as far as I was concerned; just the right amount of spiciness.

"Had you been in any of Roy Breckenridge's plays before this one?" I asked between bites.

"Oh my, no, this came as something of a surprise," she said. "He had seen me in one of the off-Broadway shows I just mentioned—a revival of Chekhov's *The Cherry Orchard* at a small theater in the Village. I played Varya, who tries to hold the family together. I'm sure you have seen it."

"I have, but it was years ago up in a smaller Canadian city," I improvised. "You must have been good to attract Breckenridge's attention."

"At the risk of seeming full of myself, I was," she said. "But it still came as a surprise when I learned that Mr. Breckenridge wanted me to read for the part of Diana Gage. I was thrilled, of course, and even more so when I got the part."

"Do you like working for him?"

She nodded but did not respond. Maybe his reputation as being a perfectionist was putting a strain on her.

I tried a different tack. "Would you say the cast members all get along with one another?"

She wrinkled her brow. "Well, I think so. At first, I was in awe of Ashley, given her great reputation, but she has been wonderful to me," she said, although her tone lacked conviction.

"What about Brad Lester? I would think given his success in Hollywood, he would be somewhat awe-inspiring as well."

"Funny that you should say that, Mr. MacGregor. I was prepared to be in awe of him every bit as much as with Ashley, but he put me at ease from the very first. He seems to totally lack any pretension. Have you talked to him?"

"Not yet. He and Max Ennis are next on my list."

"Max is a dear, an absolute dear. You will like him, I am sure of it. Now it is my turn to ask a question: Did you enjoy the show?"

"I did, and I have seen it twice now."

"I hope you write nice things about the production, and about all of us, in your magazine," she said with a smile that would melt a tray of ice cubes.

"Our goal is to give an accurate account of the plays we see, along with human-interest stories about the people in these plays," I said, feeling more like a Caleb than ever. "You are not trying to unduly influence me, are you?" I replied with a smile of my own.

"Heaven forbid, Mr. MacGregor. Would a nice girl from Lansing, Michigan, do that?"

"I simply can't imagine it. By the way, this chili is excellent, not that I ever doubted your word."

"I'm glad you like it. I hope that doesn't count as my attempt to unduly influence you."

"It does not. Let's go back to what you were saying about Max Ennis. I gather you are quite fond of him."

"Oh, I am, but not in any, well . . . inappropriate way. He has been like a favorite uncle to me, someone whose shoulder I can cry on."

"Do you do a lot of crying?"

She paused. "No . . . not really. That was just a figure of speech. What I mean is, whenever I have any questions about the play, or about New York, or anything else, I feel like I can go to him."

"Nice to have someone like that in your corner. Anything more you'd like to tell me about your experiences as part of the *Death at Cresthaven* cast?"

"Oh, I don't think so—or do you feel it is important that I should say something erudite about the role of dramatic theater in the broad and ever-changing spectrum of performing arts in America?"

"That sounds like the subject of a term paper. To be honest, it doesn't grab me, and I don't think it would grab our readers."

"I was only kidding," she said with a laugh that bordered on giggling. "And to think, I haven't even had a drink, although I never drink when I've got a performance coming up."

"That brings up another question," I said. "Do you find that there is a lot of drinking today among those working on Broadway?"

"Not that I have seen in my relatively short time in the business. Oh, I've heard stories about some of the greats over the years who had a fondness for the bottle, John Barrymore for one. But I really haven't seen any evidence of alcohol abuse since

I've been in New York. I really don't believe most actors would last very long these days if they were drunk or anywhere close to it, do you?"

"No, and I would say the same is true in Canada."

"Surprisingly, I have never been there," Melissa said, "even though it's right across the river from Detroit. And yet, when I was in college, I spent a semester in England and traveled over to Paris, too. Life is funny."

I agreed and paid the bill. "This has been very pleasant," I told Melissa as we walked back to the theater, where I still had time to talk to the other two actors before the evening performance.

# CHAPTER 13

I dropped Melissa Cartwright off at her dressing room and walked down the hall to the door marked MAX ENNIS.

"Yeah?" a voice said gruffly in response to my knock.

"It's Alan MacGregor, the magazine writer from Toronto. When you have time, I'd like to talk to you for a few minutes."

"Now is just fine for me," Ennis said, pulling open the door. "Come on in, have a seat. Mind if we do it right here in my humble abode?" he continued. "Getting around is not as easy as it used to be. After all, I'm almost eighty-two, I just seem older."

His medium-size dressing room was plain to say the least, with a pair of nondescript stuffed chairs, a scarred wooden table littered with paper plates and empty sandwich wrappers, a lumpy love seat—and of course the obligatory makeup table and mirror, neither of which appeared to have been used much by the room's current occupant.

Ennis, who wore an undershirt and jeans, had plopped

his rotund form down on the love seat, which groaned, even before I had a chance to land myself in a chair. I studied the old character actor as he wheezed and mopped a ruddy brow and a nearly bald dome with a handkerchief. "I find myself moving pretty slowly these days," he said by way of apology.

"You looked plenty energetic on the stage today," I told him, "and also when I saw a performance a few nights ago."

"Well, thank you; I am glad to hear you say so. It takes everything I've got to make it seem like I'm not straining to move around. I've been in better health, I can attest to that, and it's a good thing my role doesn't call for a lot of physical activity. Truth to tell, I feel like hell most of the time."

"You have had a fascinating career," I said, trying to steer the conversation away from Ennis's physical condition.

"I have been fortunate, darned fortunate, I'm here to tell you. And I was delighted when Roy cast me as Harley Barnes, even though, as you have seen, my character is something of a toady, which is not a role I usually play."

"Are you and Breckenridge old friends?"

"We go back a long way," he said curtly. It seemed that he was not about to elaborate.

"You said your current part is not a normal one for you. Talk about the kinds of roles you like best."

"I've been a heavy—and here I am not talking about my physique—more times than I can count. I have never been the lead, as I'm sure you know, but these tough-guy parts have been a staple for me, something I can really get my teeth into. I'm usually third or fourth billed in the program, which is fine as far as I'm concerned. I have always seemed older than my actual age. From the start, I guess I was fated to play character roles."

"And you've won a Tony," I said, using information gleaned from reading Ennis's short bio in the playbill.

"Yes, in a supporting role about ten years back as a hard-bitten, straight-talking police detective in a whodunit. The play was forgettable, but I got lucky. A reviewer from the *Times* was particularly complimentary about my role. I believe that is what really got me the award."

"I don't believe that for a minute. How do you feel about this show?"

Ennis looked at the ceiling as if mulling over the question. "It's been . . . good, a good experience."

"Any tension among the cast? And before you answer, I always ask that at least once or twice in any story I write about a show."

"Tension? Um . . . no, I wouldn't say so. Oh, there's the occasional comment after a performance about somebody not picking up a cue quickly enough or standing or sitting in the wrong place, but most of those criticisms come from either Roy or Hollis—you know, Hollis Sperry, the stage manager. They are both sticklers, which is as it should be."

"But no one-on-one trouble between actors?"

He sighed. "Okay, so I wasn't counting Ashley. I'm off the record now, understand what I'm saying?"

"I do. Believe me, I am not looking to dig up dirt. Ours is a magazine that aims to promote theater, not run it down. I suppose you could describe us as cheerleaders."

He nodded. "You know plenty about the theater world, I'm sure. So it won't come as any surprise for you to learn that Ashley can be a pain in the lower back."

"How so?"

"Sometimes, she seems to think she's the producer, director, and stage manager all rolled into one, an egomaniacal prima donna. Oh, wait—that is redundant now, isn't it, sir?"

"I will take your word for that. Sounds like Miss Williston

wouldn't win a lot of popularity contests, at least with other performers."

That brought a derisive laugh from Ennis. "I use redundancies, and you use understatement. I have only been in one other production with La Williston, and that was . . . oh, close to fifteen years back. Fortunately, we were never onstage together in that show—I might have done something violent. But I saw enough of her, both from the wings and backstage, to see what a harpy she could be. And how she browbeat others in the cast."

"Roy Breckenridge must be aware of her shortcomings," I said. "Yet he chose to cast her in this production."

"Oh, don't get me wrong, Mr. MacGregor. She is a first-rate actress when she doesn't let that hyperactive ego of hers get in the way. And on the whole, she has been pretty well behaved this time around. After all, this may well be her last chance to win a Tony, and she's lusted after one for years, which is hardly a secret around town. Although she's never said anything to me about it, I know she resents my having a Tony, even though mine was for a supporting role. And I'm sure the fact that Brad Lester has won an Oscar sticks in her craw as well."

"I haven't spoken to Mr. Lester yet. Do he and Miss Williston get along? After all, they do play a married couple."

"I suppose they get along about as well as any real-life married couple." Ennis chuckled. "Seriously, she took a couple of digs at him during rehearsals. Word is she didn't like having to share top billing with someone from *Hollywood*." Ennis made the last word sound like a disease.

"That was in rehearsals. How has their relationship played out during the run?"

"I'll throw the question back at you," Ennis said. "Do they seem natural during the performances?"

"Yes, I would say so. She is clearly the dominant one in the 'marriage,' while he seems a little . . . well, distracted and nonconfrontational. But the relationship seems realistic."

"I agree with that observation, young fella. Now backstage, it is a different matter. She treats him as though he's in the cast just to make her look good, nothing more."

"How has Mr. Lester reacted to that?"

"He has taken the high road, and if her attitude bothers him—which it damned well should—he does not let it show. You can ask him that question yourself," Ennis said, taking several deep, asthmatic breaths, as though the conversation had exhausted him.

"Maybe I will. Thank you so much for your time."

"Like I've got anything else to do between performances," he said with a dry laugh that turned into a cough. He was still coughing when I left his dressing room and closed the door behind me.

# CHAPTER 14

It was still well over an hour before curtain time, so I opted to see if I could locate the only cast member I had not yet talked to—Hollywood's own Brad Lester. My search was short, as he answered my knock on his dressing-room door. "Come in, come in, whoever you are."

I did and was greeted with a grin that showed perfect teeth. "At last! I thought maybe you were ignoring me," Lester said, rising from an ancient chair and putting out a hand. His handshake was firm, and he gestured me to a chair that was in no better shape than the one he occupied. "I can offer you only water or a second-rate beer, Mr. MacGregor," he said, smiling again.

I chose water and studied Lester. Viewed from the audience or the wings, his chiseled good looks and well-barbered black hair made him appear to be every inch the matinee idol he had been for years. Up close, he lost none of that aura. Some people seem to have it all.

"So, fire away," he said, settling back and lacing his hands behind his head. "Ask me anything, I am an open book—more or less, that is."

"I will start with an obvious question, one you've been asked many times lately I'm sure," I said, pulling out my notebook and pencil. "How difficult has the transition from screen to stage been for you?"

"Interestingly, I have not been asked that very often at all since I've been here, which has surprised me. I'll be honest, Mr. MacGregor. When I was offered this part, I was leery of accepting it. I have done almost no stage work in the past, although the theater has always fascinated me from afar, you might say. Roy Breckenridge approached my agent, who encouraged me to read for the part. I was damned nervous when I did the reading, I'll tell you that. But Roy liked what he heard, and here I am," he said, turning both palms up.

"How have the cast members accepted you? I've been told more than once that some Broadway people tend to resent what they call 'Hollywood interlopers.'"

Lester laughed and hooked one leg over the arm of the sofa, showing a finely tooled tan cowboy boot. "Oh, believe me, I have heard that as well, and I wasn't sure what to expect when I got here. But I hope I am not going to ruin a good story for your magazine. The fact is, everyone's been terrific, very supportive."

"Even Ashley Williston?"

The pause before his reply was only a second or so, but it was telling. Being a good actor, however, Lester recovered quickly. "Oh, Ashley, she has been absolutely wonderful to work with. What a professional that woman is," he said a little too quickly, waving my question away.

"I'm glad to hear that. What would you say has surprised you most about working on Broadway?"

As if searching for a reply, Lester rolled those brown eyes that had likely been setting female moviegoers' hearts aflutter for years.

"I think it is the discipline that theater people have, Mr. MacGregor, the steel nerves, really. After all, you don't get a second chance to do it right. You've got to be ready every night—and for every matinee, for that matter—and you simply can't mess up. This will hardly be a surprise to you, but I know actors out where I came from"—he made a vague gesture toward the west with his hand—"who show up in the morning totally unprepared to shoot a scene.

"And what is the result? Take after take, whole days wasted. It's no wonder half the directors in Hollywood are said to be in therapy."

"Lots of big egos, eh?"

He snorted. "More than you'd ever believe, and I think it's getting worse. It is all about discipline, and these people I'm working with have it."

"Would you say that everyone in this cast gets along well with one another?"

That brought a nod. "There is a real camaraderie, no question about it. After all, if one of us flubs a line, it ends up affecting everybody."

"Have there been many of those flubs so far?"

"No . . . not really. Oh, maybe the occasional slipup, but what few there have been were so minor that I doubt if anyone in the audience even noticed."

"How do the cast members feel about Roy Breckenridge?"

"They respect the man totally. He is a giant in the theater world, as, of course, you know better than I do, I'm sure."

"He has a great reputation, no question about it. Do you find him hard to get along with?"

"Not at all," Lester said. "Though he can be critical when he feels something isn't quite right in a performance, we often have a short meeting after a show and talk about how everything went. We are all given a chance to talk about how the performance went and what problems we saw."

"Does what gets said in these sessions ever cause friction among the cast?"

"I wouldn't say so. A little while ago, you mentioned big egos in Hollywood. Well, there are egos in the legitimate theater as well, but they don't seem to me to be as easily bruised. There has been plenty of good-natured kidding about the occasional foul-ups, but all of us, me included, take the ribbing in good spirit."

"What's the general attitude toward the stage manager?"

"Hollis Sperry? Like Mr. Breckenridge, he is definitely a stickler, a perfectionist, and he always has plenty to say when we have postperformance meetings. He can be a little more hard-hitting and acerbic in his criticisms than the producer, but his notes to the cast, and also Mr. Breckenridge's notes about what they see as missteps, are always on the mark as far as I am concerned."

"Do you feel *Cresthaven* will have a long run?"

Lester nodded. "Overall, the reviews have been good, some of them very good. And from what I've heard and been able to see, the house has been full or close to it for most of the performances. Personally, I don't have any film commitments at the moment, so I'm looking forward to a long stay in New York, a place that I find is growing on me. I'm a West Coast guy, grew up in Northern California, and I had never spent much time here before."

"Apparently, the city likes you as well, at least your performance," I told him, trying to sound like the theater booster I was supposed to be. "Do you think you will do more theater in the future?"

"I certainly would like to, Mr. MacGregor. It is energizing, and this experience has been good for me; it has helped me grow. Besides, I'm totally unfettered right now. As you may know, I've just gotten through a divorce—an amicable one, by the way. My ex-wife is an actress, and our schedules were such that we passed like ships in the night, sometimes going weeks without seeing each other. Fortunately, we never had any children."

"Well, your move into theater certainly has given you a flexibility that can only add to your marketability," I told him, again trying to sound like someone who knew what he was talking about.

"I suppose so," he said, nodding. "I'm going to be forty-nine on my next birthday—although, as you have seen, I play somebody at least ten years older in *Cresthaven*—and I know damned well that the kinds of action and adventure roles I've been lucky enough to get in Hollywood the last couple of decades will soon, very soon, start getting offered to younger actors instead; that's just the way it works, as it should. Don't get me wrong, I'm not complaining. So, faced with reality, the idea of doing more legitimate theater is very appealing to me."

"Here's to your future," I said, lifting my water glass in a salute. "Anything else you want to say to my dear Canadian readers?"

"Drop everything you're doing in Ottawa or Montreal or wherever you live, book a flight to New York immediately, and see *Death at Cresthaven*. How does that sound?"

"It sounds like someone who could have had himself a career as an advertising copywriter," I said.

Lester laughed. "Thanks anyway, but I'll stick to the worlds of celluloid and greasepaint. Speaking of greasepaint," he said, looking at his watch, "I'd better start getting into character to play the somewhat vague and absentminded Carlisle Mills.

Next time you see me, this hair will be salt-and-pepper, and I'll be hunched over and slightly shuffling, as well as acting somewhat vague."

"I'll leave you to it. Thanks for your time," I told him as I left his dressing room.

# CHAPTER 15

Walking along the basement hall of the old theater, I felt frustrated and more than a little useless. I had now spent some time with all the principals involved in *Death at Cresthaven*, and if there was some deep, dark plot or intrigue, as Roy Breckenridge had suggested, I failed to see it.

There was a possibility, of course, that one or more of the cast had lied to me about the chemistry or attitudes among the troupe. After all, these people are skilled at wearing masks and playing at being characters they weren't. And I reluctantly conceded the likelihood that I had not asked probing enough questions of them.

But then, I was wearing a mask of my own: that of an ever-so-earnest reporter-writer for a fictitious Canadian arts magazine who also had to stay in character. If I, as a self-professed cheerleader for the theater world, began probing too pointedly about who disliked whom in the cast, I would have been seen as a potential scandalmonger, and everyone would have clammed up. I had not liked this idea from the beginning, but once Wolfe committed me, I gave it what I felt was my best shot.

I would watch tonight's performance, just so that I could say I had seen the show three times, and in the morning, I would tell Wolfe we were wasting Breckenridge's money. Satisfied with my decision, I took my place in the wings at stage left with pencil and notebook in hand to continue my charade.

The performance was the best of the three I had seen so far. The actors seemed energized; maybe either Breckenridge or Sperry—or both—had given them a pep talk. Or perhaps they were growing progressively more comfortable with their roles. Whatever the reasons, the show moved along at a brisk pace, and Ashley Williston, in particular, was in top form as she writhed and died of strangulation delivered in the parlor by Max Ennis, playing the neighbor who loved her and found that she felt nothing more for him than pity.

As the cast took their collective bow, I noticed that both Ashley and Melissa Cartwright looked unusually animated, the color in their cheeks indicating to me an enthusiasm over a successful evening. Even old Max Ennis, the murderer, allowed himself a brief out-of-character grin when he urged the audience to keep the play's ending a secret from future theatergoers.

As the curtain came down and the applause subsided, the cast headed for their dressing rooms. The stagehands quickly scrambled onto the set to begin putting it in order for the next performance. I tucked my notebook in my breast pocket and walked across the stage toward the booth from which Breckenridge had been watching the performance.

Hollis Sperry got there before me, knocked on the booth door, and poked his head in. When he emerged, his face was a study in terror, eyes and mouth wide. He started to say something, but no sound came out.

In response to my "What is it?" he jabbed an index finger at the interior of the booth, still silent. I looked inside and saw Breckenridge slumped on the small desk just below the window that looked out onto the stage. His head was turned toward me, eyes and mouth open, face ashen. I loosened his collar and pressed my fingers against his carotid. He was gone.

"Call the police!" I barked at Sperry, who came out of his trance and turned, loping toward the pay phone at the stage door. The stagehands went about their business, unaware of what had happened, which was fine by me for the moment. I left the theater in search of a telephone, finding a booth half a block west on the corner of Eighth Avenue. I dialed the number I know best.

"Yes?" Wolfe snapped. He has no interest whatever in telephone etiquette.

"Me. We don't have a client anymore." I succinctly fed him the details.

"Confound it, where are you?"

I told him.

"Come home immediately."

That was one order I was happy to follow, and after a ten-minute cab ride, I walked into the office. Wolfe set his book down and glared at me.

I glared back and sat at my desk. "What a fine kettle of fish we find ourselves in here," I said.

"This is hardly a time for banalities," Wolfe grumped, draining the last of the beer in his glass. "You gave me a précis when you called. What more can you add?"

"Not a lot, I am sorry to say. I watched two performances from backstage today, but I failed miserably in one respect:

I can't even tell you who might have entered Breckenridge's little booth during the evening show. I was too occupied watching the action onstage. I am willing to hand in my resignation. Maybe Del Bascom will rehire me to work for his agency. I understand his business is good, and he's been adding to his payroll lately. And as you have said before, Bascom is a good man."

"Enough! Did you have any reason to suspect Mr. Breckenridge was in mortal peril?"

"No. And I realize of course that I haven't talked to you about my interviews with the members of the cast and the stage manager. Would you like me to unload now?"

Wolfe scowled, eyeing the wall clock and looking down at his closed book. "Very well, report."

For the next hour, I gave him a rundown on my conversations with each of the principals. I didn't consult my notes, simply because I had not taken any. The notebook was just a sham. As I related the conversations, Wolfe listened, eyes closed, with his fingers interlaced over his middle mound. When I finished, he blinked once and came forward in his chair.

"No one of them was overly forthcoming," he remarked.

"I blame myself. I was trying too hard to play the wide-eyed theater enthusiast whose job was to promote the business. I did not ask probing questions or I might have discovered that someone had it in for Roy Breckenridge."

"You were placed in a difficult position," Wolfe conceded. "Also, we do not yet know how Mr. Breckenridge died. Is it possible he had a heart condition?"

"Could be, I suppose."

"If he did not die of natural causes, it is likely we shall soon be hearing from Mr. Cramer."

Wolfe was referring to Inspector Lionel T. Cramer, head

of the New York Police Department's Homicide Squad and a longtime acquaintance of ours.

"What makes you think Cramer will want to talk to us?"

"Come now, Archie," Wolfe chided. "We must be prepared. Mr. Alan MacGregor, representing what turns out to be a fictitious Canadian theater magazine, suddenly disappears after Mr. Breckenridge's death. The police, of course, will interview members of the cast and staff about the suspicious MacGregor, and they will surely get one of their artists to sketch a likeness—of you."

"Yeah, as much as I hate to admit it, you have got a point. How do we play things from here on?"

Before Wolfe could respond, the phone rang, and I answered. It was Lon Cohen.

"You have got some explaining to do," he barked as I nodded to Wolfe, who picked up his receiver.

"Is that so? Explaining about what?"

"Don't play dumb, it does not become you. We just got word that Roy Breckenridge was found dead in the theater after tonight's performance. That is the selfsame Roy Breckenridge you asked me to get you some information about just days ago. What would you like to tell me?"

"I am on the line, Mr. Cohen," Wolfe said. "Has the cause of Mr. Breckenridge's death been determined?"

"Not yet, as far as I know. Was he a client?"

"I am not prepared to respond at present, but be assured that at such time as we have something concrete to report, you will be the first person we telephone."

"But can't you give me something now?" Lon said in a pleading tone.

"No sir, I cannot," Wolfe said, cradling his instrument, which left me to placate Lon. "You heard Mr. Wolfe," I told him. "We have always been square and given you the goods first, before talking to any other paper. It will be the same this time—that is, if we ever do have anything to tell you."

"You have not heard the last of me on this, Archie," he snapped.

"When have I ever heard the last of you involving anything?" I shot back, and we terminated the conversation.

# CHAPTER 16

I did not have to wait long to hear from Lon Cohen again. The next morning, I had just settled in at my desk in the office with a postbreakfast coffee when the telephone made its usual sound.

"I am sitting at my desk holding a copy of the *Daily News*, a paper I know you and Mr. Wolfe will not deign to soil your hands on. However, today's edition might interest you."

"Really? I did not realize you were a fan of the tabloid that calls itself 'New York's Picture Newspaper.'"

"I always read the competition, whatever I may think of it; you never know what you might find. Like this morning, for instance."

"Well, don't keep me in suspense. Out with it."

"I might make fun of the *Daily News* sometimes, but I have got to hand it to them. Those guys are bulldogs when it comes to knowing how to play a big story."

"As in the death of Roy Breckenridge?"

"Exactly. First off, and we got this from the police, too, he died from a healthy—or I should say unhealthy—dose of arsenic in his Coca-Cola."

"A poison that is highly soluble in liquid and easy to get hold of."

"Right, as in rat poison, of course. So we'll have it in our early editions, too. But we won't have something that is in the *News*."

"Stop playing games, dammit."

"Okay, they have got a sidebar to the main story about Breckenridge's death headlined 'Have You Seen Mister Canadian?' It seems that a man calling himself Alan MacGregor was on the set of *Death at Cresthaven* nosing around and interviewing the cast for the last day or so. He represented himself as a writer for a Toronto magazine called *StageArts Canada*, which, as it turns out, does not exist. Suspicious, wouldn't you say?"

"I suppose so."

"But wait, there's more. The sidebar includes a police artist's facial sketch of the man said to be Alan MacGregor. Now, you and I both know these sketches are usually generic and bland, especially since the people supplying the details don't all agree on exactly what the individual in question looks like."

"What's your point, Lon?"

"The point is, the sketch in the *Daily News* seems to look somewhat like you."

"I am sad to say there are plenty of people around who resemble me, and I do not envy them their bad fortune."

"Perhaps, but I have to wonder how many of these so-called Archie Goodwin 'look-alikes' have been seeking information about Roy Breckenridge."

"I think we have exhausted the subject for now," I said.

"It's not going away, Archie, you can bank on that. Stiff me if you want to, but be prepared for more questions, very possibly from Inspector Cramer. This is one big story, and the heat is on the cops, which is hardly a surprise. I don't have to tell you how important theater is in this town. It is one of the engines that generates the big bucks, not just for the theaters, but for the hotels and airlines and restaurants and cabbies. Trouble on Broadway means trouble for the whole city. If you don't believe me, just ask the mayor."

"There we have one fine speech, Mister Deadline, I will give you that. I almost stood up and saluted. Now, if you'll excuse me, I must serve the needs of the man who signs my checks." After hanging up, I took a deep breath. Lon had a point, and I knew it.

I typed several letters Wolfe had dictated the day before, finishing the last one just before I heard the elevator bring the boss down from the plant rooms. No sooner than he had asked if I had slept well and settled in behind his desk, the doorbell rang. I went to the hall, and through the one-way glass in the front door, I saw a familiar bulky figure.

"Good morning, Inspector," I said. "What brings you around on this fine August morning?"

"I will tell you when we have a fine morning, and this is not one of them," Cramer snorted, gripping a crumpled newspaper in his hand, charging by me and heading toward the office under a full head of steam. By the time I got there, he had dropped into the red leather chair and pulled a cigar from his breast pocket.

Wolfe, who had just rung for beer, considered his uninvited guest with raised eyebrows but said nothing.

Cramer smoothed out the newspaper—it was that morning's *Daily News*—and slapped it down on the desk blotter. "See that sketch?" he said, jabbing a thick finger at the page. "Does it remind you of anyone?"

Wolfe peered at it, and so did I, moving around behind him to get a better look. "The gentleman, whoever he is, appears to be somewhat bland," Wolfe said airily.

"Bland, my aunt Betsy!" the inspector blurted. "You don't even recognize your own employee?"

"Mr. Cramer, if you please. You barge into my home unannounced, which I realize is hardly unprecedented, and you throw a newspaper at me, demanding I identify the man in an amateurish drawing. This is twaddle!"

"I will give you twaddle, Wolfe. Sergeant Stebbins showed me the paper this morning and said 'Whose picture is that?'

"'Looks a lot like Goodwin,' I said, and he answered 'Damned right it does. Let's run him in.' Now, I know how the two of you feel about Purley Stebbins, and I admit he can be abrasive sometimes, so I'm doing you a favor by not having him come here with me. I thought we could talk this out, the three of us."

"What is there to talk about, Mr. Cramer?" Wolfe said, opening the first of two beers Fritz had placed before him. "Archie, do you recognize that sketch as being your likeness?"

"I flatter myself by thinking that I look a lot better than this poor schnook, whoever he is," I said.

"So there we are," Wolfe said, spreading his hands, palms down, on the desk.

"I could of course compel Goodwin to be part of a lineup downtown and have the cast of that play see if they could identify you," Cramer said. "But I know damned well that you would then call your conspirator Cohen at the *Gazette* and charge police harassment, which would get spread all over that rag's pages."

"It seems to me we are getting ahead of ourselves, Mr. Cramer," Wolfe said calmly. "We have read in this morning's *Times* about the unfortunate event at the theater last night. What makes you think Archie was in any way involved?"

"Whenever there's trouble in New York, and this business is big trouble, the two of you are invariably involved."

"That is patent nonsense, sir, and you well know it," Wolfe said.

"If you have got several hours to spare, I can list all the times you have gotten in the way of an investigation."

"Perhaps you also can enumerate all the occasions in which Archie and I have contributed to the resolution of a case that had you and the rest of the police department flummoxed," Wolfe fired back.

That drew a glower from the inspector, who stood, threw his unlit cigar at the wastebasket, and picked up his fedora. "Balls! I might have known the kind of cooperation—or rather, lack of it—I'd get around here." With that, he stormed out, leaving me to dispose of the chewed-on stogie on the carpet a foot from the dustbin.

After Cramer had departed, I asked Wolfe, "What now, boss?" He hates it when I call him that, but in my current mood, I didn't much care about his feelings.

"Call Mr. Hewitt," he murmured.

"Oh, now I get it. One client dies on us and we get another one, right?"

He threw me a glare that would have cowed a lesser man, but I merely shrugged. "If I reach him, should I stay on the line?" His response was the half-inch dip of the chin that passes for a nod.

I dialed Hewitt's Long Island home, and a lackey of the male species answered. I identified myself as calling for Nero Wolfe, and he told me in a supercilious tone that "I will endeavor to locate Mr. Hewitt, who currently is somewhere on the property."

Apparently, the lackey was able to locate the lord of the manor within five minutes, and I nodded back at Wolfe, who picked up his receiver.

"Mr. Wolfe, you beat me to it; I was about to call you," Hewitt said. The two men have known each other for years, and their relationship, despite their fierce competition in the orchid world, has been a cordial one. However, neither has ever called the other by his first name. I guess that is what is called "old school."

"You know, of course, of yesterday's events," Wolfe said.

"I do, and I am saddened beyond words," Hewitt said. "With your permission, I would like to pay you a visit."

"Come for dinner tonight, Mr. Hewitt. We are having shrimp bordelaise."

"Oh, please, do not think it was my intention to invite myself to break bread at your table, sir."

"That never entered my mind," Wolfe replied. "It has been some time since we dined together, and I would be honored to have you here as our guest."

"In that case, I accept. We have a good deal to discuss."

"We do indeed."


At ten until seven, our bell sounded, and I went to the front door to admit Lewis Hewitt.

"Good evening, Mr. Goodwin," he said with a smile, shaking hands. "It has been some time since I have seen you."

Hewitt is a big man, over six feet, and with substantial girth, although hardly in Wolfe's class. Well traveled and urbane, he makes an engaging dinner guest, as he can converse on a wide range of subjects.

I led him directly to the dining room, where Wolfe was just getting seated. They exchanged pleasantries, and Fritz served the first course, celery and cantaloupe salad.

As usual, Wolfe set the meal topic, which, on this occasion, was the reason the Whig Party disappeared from the American political scene in the mid-nineteenth century. I long ago accepted Wolfe's ironclad rule that business was not to be discussed during meals, but that did not keep me from becoming antsy throughout dinner. After all, according to the *Daily News* sketch, I resembled the mysterious "Mister Canadian," a prime suspect in the death of Roy Breckenridge, so I was anxious that Wolfe get cracking.

Finally, after we had consumed generous wedges of blueberry pie à la mode, and Hewitt had heaped praise on Fritz, we moved to the office for coffee and Remisier.

"This is the nectar of the gods," Hewitt said, holding up his snifter after savoring his first sip of the rare cognac. "It is almost enough to make me forget about the tragedy that befell Roy."

"You had known Mr. Breckenridge well," Wolfe stated.

"Well—yes, yes I had. As you are aware, I have had an interest in theater for a long time, and I first met Roy, oh, probably twenty years ago now, at a premiere party of one of the plays he produced, a period piece set at the time of the Regency in England. I had liked it very much and said so, and then he told me about his next project, a revival of Eugene O'Neill's *Desire Under the Elms*. That has always been a favorite of mine, and I said that if he needed any financial backing for the production, he could count on me."

"May I assume he accepted your offer?"

"You may. He was absolutely delighted, and almost from that moment, we formed what you might call an informal partnership. In the ensuing years, I've been a backer of several of his productions, including *Death at Cresthaven*."

"Were your financial contributions essential to the plays being produced?" Wolfe asked.

"Oh, I suppose they helped a good deal," Hewitt said, flipping a palm, "but I never was the only backer of these productions; there always were several of us, including Roy himself. That is one of the things I liked about him: He was always willing to support his ideas with his own money."

"Was he wealthy?"

"He certainly lived well. Speaking of money, Mr. Wolfe, I know Roy had hired you—at my suggestion—to look into whatever was concerning him at the production, and the main reason I wanted to see you is to take over his role as client. You may set whatever fee you wish. I want to see whoever did this caught and convicted."

"The financial arrangements can wait," Wolfe said. "How much did Mr. Breckenridge tell you about our investigation?"

"Nothing, other than that you had agreed to look into whatever was bothering him so much."

"What I am about to tell you must remain between us, at least for the present."

"I have been known to be most tight-lipped," Hewitt said.

"Very well. At Mr. Breckenridge's suggestion, Archie masqueraded as a reporter for a Canadian art magazine and—"

"So he is the mysterious 'Mister Canadian' the newspapers have been writing about?"

"Yes, sir, he is. And for now, we wish him to remain mysterious—and anonymous."

"You may rely on me."

"Had you seen *Death at Cresthaven*?" Wolfe asked.

"Yes, on opening night. I liked it, although not as much as some of Roy's other productions. However, it is not always a good idea to judge the quality of a show on its premiere. I understand from others that it has since improved."

"You stated earlier that you had no idea as to the reasons for Mr. Breckenridge's angst."

"That is correct. But it was obvious from a telephone conversation we had that he was extremely unnerved, which was not like the man. He always has seemed to me to be self-possessed and in control."

"What else can you tell Mr. Goodwin and me about him?"

Hewitt poured another snifter of Remisier from the bottle I had placed on the small table next to his chair. "This will sound like a cliché, but I don't know how else to phrase it: He lived life to the fullest. He enjoyed fine food and wine, elaborate parties—whether he was host or guest—exotic vacations, and beautiful women of all ages. He was married to three of them."

"And also divorced three times?" I asked.

Hewitt nodded. "He certainly was not a faithful husband by most definitions of the institution of marriage, although he was surely a generous mate. He lavished furs and jewelry on his wives and escorted them to all manner of galas both here and abroad. But I always got the feeling that he saw them more as prized possessions than as cherished spouses."

Wolfe scowled. "Do you know any of the members of the *Death at Cresthaven* cast?"

"A few of them. Everybody who has had anything to do with the Broadway theater world in the last twenty-plus years knows Ashley Williston, of course. She has been around the block and makes sure that she gets to know everyone she thinks can help further her career."

"You suggest she is an opportunist?"

That brought a hearty laugh from Hewitt. "To say the least! I have often seen her at parties, buttonholing critics, editors on the newspapers, press agents, even secretaries to press agents. It has gotten to the point where people at social gatherings say they 'got Ashley-ed' the other night, meaning she cornered them and extolled her acting qualities."

"You have scant respect for her abilities?" Wolfe posed.

"Actually, the woman is not bad, albeit often overly dramatic. But it eats at her that she has never won a Tony Award. I believe that she would go to almost any lengths to get one."

"Literally?" I asked.

"Oh no, pardon my hyperbole. Chalk it up to the tongue-loosening qualities of this wonderful cognac," Hewitt said, turning to Wolfe. "Moving on, you asked who I knew in the cast, and the only other one I've met is Max Ennis, who has been around even longer than Ashley."

Wolfe paused to drink beer. "Your opinion of him?"

"A true professional. His list of credits is as long as your arm, although he has never been a star. But every producer, director, and stage manager on Broadway, and off-Broadway for that matter, knows that if Max is in the cast, they will get a solid performance."

"Do you think either he or Miss Williston would have any reason to kill Roy Breckenridge?"

"I can't begin to conceive it," Hewitt said. "Unthinkable."

"Can you suggest any other candidates?"

"I cannot. And I am not about to wait for the police to find a killer. I would like to hire you to find that individual. Let us discuss your fee, and I will pay even if you are unsuccessful, which I think unlikely."

"I seek no money from you," Wolfe said.

Hewitt jerked upright. "Really?"

"Really. Do you remember the two words you spoke to Mr. Goodwin when you first called here to enlist my help regarding Mr. Breckenridge?"

"I don't think I can recall them. . . ." Hewitt said, although I did not for a moment believe him.

"Let me refresh your memory. The words were *Grammangis spectabilis.*"

Hewitt grinned and threw up his arms. "All right, I surrender. I have six of them. I can give you two."

"Three," Wolfe said.

"These are rare beyond words," Hewitt protested.

"As am I, sir, in my field."

Our guest took a deep breath and exhaled. "You drive a hard bargain, sir," he said.

"I do not think so. I considered asking for four."

## CHAPTER 17

"Well, you got exactly what you wanted," I told Wolfe when I returned to the office after seeing Hewitt out. "Where do we go from here?"

"We call Inspector Cramer."

"Why? He already suspects that I am the mystery man."

"We are going to confirm that fact to him," Wolfe said, finishing his beer and dabbing his lips with a handkerchief.

"Well, isn't that just great now? Would you suggest that I pack now for my stay behind bars?"

"Archie, you know as well as I do that, sooner rather than later, your charade will come to light, and it befits us to take the initiative."

"If I may be so bold as to remind you, this charade, to use your term, was one you agreed to after Breckenridge proposed it. This was not—repeat *not*—my idea."

"Point taken. Given subsequent events, such was perhaps ill-advised. But we must live with the world as it is, not as we would wish it."

"Very cute. I suppose that's Shakespeare."

"No, it comes from me. Is now too late to telephone Mr. Cramer at home?"

I checked my watch. "Nine thirty? No, he will still be up. He once told me he's a night owl who reads a lot. Do you want him to come here tonight?"

"No—in the morning. Dial his number and I will speak with him."

The inspector's wife picked up, and I stayed on the line. "Mrs. Cramer, this is Nero Wolfe. Is the inspector available?"

"Just a minute, please," she said in a calm tone. If she was surprised by the caller, it was not reflected in her voice.

"Wolfe!" he rasped, "don't tell me that you're pulling one of your 'I'm going to name the killer' stunts tonight. This is pretty damned short notice."

"No sir, such is not my intention. I am calling to ask if you could come to my home tomorrow morning at eleven to discuss the death of Mr. Breckenridge."

"What are you up to?" Cramer growled. "I can't remember the last time you called me at home at night."

"I apologize for the intrusion, sir. However, I felt I should extend the invitation as soon as possible."

"Who else will be there with us?"

"Only Archie."

Cramer exhaled. "All right, I'll come, but it better be worth my while."

"You can be the judge of that after we have spoken," Wolfe said, and we all hung up.

"So I get thrown to the wolves, or actually *by* the Wolfe," I said. My boss scowled at my cheap attempt at humor.

\* \* \*

The next morning at eleven, the doorbell rang, and I went to the front hall to admit the inspector. He glowered but said nothing, bulling past me and heading for the office like a locomotive with a green signal. He arrived there just as Wolfe was entering after his morning session upstairs with the orchids.

"Would you like something to drink, sir? I will have beer," Wolfe said as he settled in behind his desk.

"Of course you will," Cramer growled, planting himself in the red leather chair as if he owned it and pulling out a cigar, which he jammed unlit into his mouth as usual. "Nothing for me, thanks. Now, just why am I here?"

"That sketch you brought us that ran in the *Daily News*, it was of Archie."

"Dammit, I can't believe I'm hearing this!" Cramer roared, rising partway out of the chair and then slamming himself back down. "This better be good, and I mean really good."

"Hear me out, please," Wolfe said calmly, holding up a hand as Fritz placed two chilled bottles of beer and a glass in front of him. "We were approached by Roy Breckenridge, who told us he had some unformed concerns about the show he was producing and directing. He felt he needed someone in the theater to be his eyes and ears."

Wolfe then proceeded to describe my role and actions, as well as the events that transpired right up to Breckenridge's death and my leaving the theater in a hurry.

The inspector's jaw dropped, and his mouth stayed open during Wolfe's recitation. Three times, he looked like he wanted to speak, but nothing came out. When Wolfe finished and Cramer finally spoke, his voice was hoarse, as if he had been shouting.

"I am trying to count the number of charges I could run both of you in on," he said, spacing the words in an admirable attempt to keep from losing his well-known temper. "This is a travesty."

"A travesty? I think not, sir," Wolfe said. "Were we remiss in not communicating with you sooner? Perhaps. However, Archie and I have broken no laws, committed no crimes. My regret, and it is manifest, is that an individual came to us seeking help, and we failed him."

"Nuts!" Cramer barked. "Be honest. Your biggest regret is that you lost a client—and a payday in the process."

"Your reaction is understandable, sir, and I will not cavil. The question is: Where do we go from here? And I have a suggestion. Are you interested in hearing it?"

"Oh, what the hell!" Cramer said, throwing up his hands in disgust. "Why not?"

"Very well. It is our intention to work with the police. I believe you will agree with me that Archie is a keen observer and a perceptive interviewer. During his time at the theater, he—"

"He passed himself off as a Canadian magazine writer," Cramer said.

"We already have stipulated that," Wolfe said. "Are you to tell me that no detective in the employ of the New York Police Department has ever misrepresented himself in the line of duty? Archie well may be—"

"That is a totally different matter," the inspector cut in defiantly.

"Is it? We can leave that discussion for another time. I started to say, before I was interrupted, that Archie may well be of help to you. As I mentioned earlier, he spoke at length to each of the cast members as well as to the stage manager and to Breckenridge himself. I suggest that Archie make himself available to someone in your employ—and *not* Lieutenant Rowcliff—for questioning."

"Listen, Wolfe, you know that I could drag him in right now, just like that," Cramer said, snapping his fingers.

"You could," Wolfe conceded, "but knowing Archie as I do, I believe he would become mute under those circumstances, and you would then get nothing."

"He might open up after he spent some time cooling his heels as our guest," Cramer replied. The inspector set his jaw, but I could tell he was weakening. "All right," he said. "We have got a lieutenant that neither of you has ever met, name of Sievers. I am told that he is one damned good interviewer. If Goodwin has some useful information, Sievers will get it."

It was a strange feeling, watching the two of them discussing me as if I weren't in the room. "Do I have any say-so in all of this?" I asked. That resulted in glares from both Wolfe and Cramer.

"All right then, put me down as eager to meet the brilliant Lieutenant Sievers," I told them.

"Not so fast," Cramer cut in. "Before we go one step further, I want everything kept out of the newspapers for the present, and that includes your buddy Cohen at the *Gazette*. I know how you love to feed him scoops, but if one word of Goodwin's role in all this gets out, I swear you both will get hauled in."

"Inspector, you have my word that neither Archie nor I will discuss Mr. Breckenridge's death or Archie's role as a Canadian journalist with Mr. Cohen or with any other member of the press at the present time," Wolfe said.

"Just what does 'at the present time' mean?"

"It means that your Lieutenant Sievers may interview Archie without any interference from me. I will not inform Mr. Cohen or any other journalist of this interview. However, if someone on the police force chooses to leak information about the meeting, such is beyond my governance and I will react accordingly."

"If there is a leak in the department, that falls within my . . . what did you call it . . . governance? And by God, if that happens, someone will pay for it," Cramer barked, slapping a palm on the arm of the red leather chair.

"Understood," Wolfe said. "One stipulation: Messrs. Rowcliff and Stebbins are not to be present during Archie's conversation with Lieutenant Sievers." Wolfe was referring to the stuttering Lieutenant George Rowcliff, who didn't like me any more than I liked him, and Sergeant Purley Stebbins, Cramer's sidekick, who both Wolfe and I agreed was capable in his limited way but had always been antagonistic toward us.

"All right." Cramer exhaled. "Any other monkey wrenches that you want to throw in before we move on?"

"This request hardly throws a monkey wrench into the works, sir," Wolfe responded. "I merely am attempting to ensure that this meeting goes as smoothly as possible, for everyone's sake."

"I certainly appreciate your concern. I will be calling to let you know when we expect Goodwin at headquarters," the inspector said, rising.

"Before you leave, I have another question, sir," Wolfe said.

"Of course you do. Now what?"

"May I assume you and your men searched Mr. Breckenridge's home?"

"Of course we did," Cramer barked.

"And did you find anything of interest?"

"That's actually two questions—so far."

"Humor me, please," Wolfe said. "We have been candid with you today."

The inspector let out a protracted sigh. "What I am about to say must remain in this office."

"Understood."

"There were three notes, all of them folded up in the drawer of a nightstand in Breckenridge's bedroom."

"Indeed. What was the content?"

"Pretty much the same on each of the messages: 'Stop your evil actions immediately,' and 'If you do not cease your sinful behavior, you will pay dearly,' and the third was similar. I may be paraphrasing slightly, but that was the essence. They all were printed in block letters in ink on cheap stationery, the kind you could buy at any dime store. We dusted them for prints, and the only ones were Breckenridge's."

"Did you or your men mention these notes to the others involved in the production?"

"We did not. And we haven't told anyone in the press, either. Nor will you," Cramer said in an ominous tone.

"Agreed, sir," Wolfe replied evenly.

Cramer rose to leave a second time, his jaw set as he turned to me. "I hope you enjoy your time with Lieutenant Sievers," he said before marching down the hall to the front door.

# CHAPTER 18

The call came that afternoon when Wolfe was up in the plant rooms, although it was not from Cramer. A woman whose nasal tone had New Jersey flavorings informed me that "Lieutenant Sievers of Homicide expects you promptly at nine thirty tomorrow morning in room 411 at One Police Plaza. That is One Police Plaza. Nine thirty. Room 411." She finished by snapping, "Do you have that information?"

I told her I did, and she urged me to "make sure that you are on time." I started to ask her if she had ever taught fourth grade, but the line went dead. Perhaps she had gone on to bedevil someone else.

I have never liked One Police Plaza, a cold, square, hard-edged building down near the Brooklyn Bridge and done in a style referred to as "brutalist" by Lon Cohen, who is conversant on architecture, among myriad other things. But then, I never liked its predecessor at 240 Centre Street either, which was older and of a totally different design. I must be allergic to police stations.

The woman with the Jersey accent would have been pleased to know that I arrived at One Police Plaza at 9:10, well-fed, freshly shaved, and wearing a suit and tie. Seated behind a desk in the lobby, a uniform who didn't look like he was old enough to vote took my name and checked it against a list, then gestured me to a bank of elevators. I managed to locate room 411 and knocked, getting a crisp "Come in!"

The windowless room contained a metal table; three metal chairs; a man, standing; and a woman, seated. "You would be Goodwin," the man said, and I nodded. "I am Wesley Sievers, and this young woman is the stenographer, as you can see from the device in front of her. Do you have any questions before we start?"

I said no, and he gestured me to one of the chairs while he took another on the opposite side of the table. Sievers wore a serviceable dark business suit that I would call "standard-issue police-detective style." He was tall, lean, and in his mid to late thirties, and he had a strong jaw, blue eyes, and close-cropped brown hair. He reminded me of a colonel I had known in my army days.

The stenographer, who I later learned was named Jeannette, was the only adornment in an otherwise drab room. Slender and in her twenties, she had a face worth memorizing—brown eyes, high cheekbones, a cute nose that just missed being turned up, and center-parted auburn hair. She looked like the type who smiled easily and often, although she wore a serious expression as befitted the occasion.

Sievers cleared his throat. "Before we go on, Goodwin, you should know that I have little if any use for what you and your ilk like to term yourselves, 'private investigators.' To me, you are no more than a motley collection of keyhole peepers and ambulance chasers looking to make a fast and easy buck while getting in the way of the duly commissioned officers of the law."

"You are entitled to your opinion," I answered, deadpan.

"So I am," Sievers said. "Now that you know where I stand, I will say that you will be treated fairly by me."

"That is good to know."

"Okay, let's get right to it," Sievers said when my eyes lingered a beat too long on Jeannette's visage. "This interview with Mr. Archie Goodwin of Nero Wolfe's detective office commences at oh-nine-twenty-seven," he said, addressing the steno.

"All right, Mr. Goodwin, explain how you came to be impersonating a Canadian journalist named Alan MacGregor on the set of the Broadway production *Death at Cresthaven*."

Wolfe had said to leave nothing out, so I took Sievers from the time Hewitt called us to ask that we see Roy Breckenridge on through to when Breckenridge's body was found. Sievers interrupted several times with questions, including "Have you ever impersonated a magazine writer before?" (No) and "Are you conversant with the workings of the Broadway theater?" (No) to "Had you previously met any of the members of the play's cast and crew?" (No).

Here is a further example of the morning's session:

> **W.S.:** Would you say that you are a student of human nature?
>
> **A.G.:** As much as anyone, I suppose.
>
> **W.S.:** Come, come, Mr. Goodwin. As a longtime private investigator, you surely have had numerous opportunities to interrogate a wide variety of individuals and gauge their responses.
>
> **A.G.:** That is true.

**W.S.:** We know, of course, that you spent time one-on-one with each of the cast members of *Death at Cresthaven*, as well as with the play's stage manager, Mr. Hollis Sperry. Given your wealth of experience, did you draw any conclusions as to the possible murderer of Mr. Breckenridge?

**A.G.:** I did not.

**W.S.:** Really? When you reported back to Nero Wolfe, did you not suggest to him a likely candidate as the killer?

**A.G.:** I did not.

**W.S.:** Is it not true that you and Nero Wolfe were hired by Mr. Breckenridge because he was fearful of something or someone?

**A.G.:** Yes.

**W.S.:** Did he tell you what or whom he was fearful of?

**A.G.:** He did not.

**W.S.:** Did you, as a seasoned private investigator, ask him for specifics?

**A.G.:** I did, but he seemed unable to articulate the nature of his fears.

**W.S.:** Would you say that you were a failure in this endeavor?

**A.G.:** I had not yet completed my investigation at the time of Mr. Breckenridge's death.

**W.S.:** Do you think it is likely that if you had had more time, you might have identified a potential killer?

**A.G.:** We will never know.

**W.S.:** So true, Mr. Goodwin. You were among those who discovered Mr. Breckenridge's body after the performance. Yet you did not choose to inform the police. Why?

**A.G.:** Mr. Sperry, the stage manager, already had gone to call them.

**W.S.:** At your urging, as I understand it. And then you left the scene. As a duly licensed P.I. in the state of New York, you had a responsibility to remain at the crime scene. Your actions could very well endanger your license.

**A.G.:** I exercised bad judgment in the heat of the moment.

**W.S.:** I could not have said it better, Mr. Goodwin. Do you have anything else to add that could aid the police in the investigation of Mr. Breckenridge's death?

**A.G.:** No, sir.

**W.S.:** (Scowling) Interview terminated at oh-nine-fifty-three.

"This has been one colossal waste of time," Sievers snarled as he rose to leave. "If it were my call, I would pull your license so fast you wouldn't even realize it was missing. However, that is in the hands of people at a higher level than mine, so it is possible that you may get by with this."

I had no response, so I merely grinned at Jeannette, who sent me the hint of a smile in return. Apparently, she was not as repulsed by my presence as was Lieutenant Wesley Sievers.

I was back at my desk in the office when Wolfe came down from the plant rooms at eleven. Once he got settled, riffled through the morning mail, and rang for beer, I gave him a verbatim account of my visit to One Police Plaza. "It will not go down as one of my shining moments," I said.

He moved his shoulders slightly in his version of a shrug. "No matter. We have shown all our cards to Inspector Cramer and his minion. He cannot accuse us of being furtive."

"I suppose that is true, but there remains the issue of my license. He could very well pull it."

"Pah!" Wolfe said, flipping a palm dismissively. "Although he will never admit it, the inspector finds us useful. He knows that were he to do that, we would cease to cooperate with him, not just on this case, but on future ones as well. Do you feel it fair to say we have aided him immeasurably over the years?"

"There's no question about it."

"Not only that," Wolfe continued, "but we have, in most instances, shunned the spotlight and let the police department in general and Inspector Cramer in particular take the credit. I believe your license to be safe."

"I will take solace in that. Where do we go from here?"

Wolfe was about to answer when the telephone rang. I picked up the receiver. "Nero Wolfe's office, Archie Good—"

"Yeah, yeah, enough with the formalities," Lon Cohen said. "Still interested in the Breckenridge murder, for whatever reasons you don't choose to share with me?"

"Why do you ask?" I replied, nodding to Wolfe to pick up his instrument.

"Because of something we just got from our man in the press room at police headquarters. One of the members of the cast in his play just tried to commit suicide and is on life support at New York Hospital."

"Mr. Cohen, this is Nero Wolfe. What has happened?"

"According to the police, Max Ennis, who has been playing Harley Barnes in *Death at Cresthaven*, took a dose of arsenic at his flat in Greenwich Village and is in a coma. He probably would have been a goner, except that he hit the floor, apparently after taking the poison, and the woman in the apartment below him heard the thud. Then, after banging on his door and getting no response, she quickly called the cops."

"Did Mr. Ennis leave a note?" Wolfe asked.

"Sort of. A scrap of paper on an end table near where he had fallen contained just two words, printed in pencil: 'I'm sorry.' The police, no surprise, feel they have identified Roy Breckenridge's killer, especially because the same poison was used on both men."

"No doubt," Wolfe said. "It would initially appear that Mr. Ennis has done their work for them."

"Yeah, so it would seem," Lon replied. "There must have been bad blood between Breckenridge and Ennis. I know you and Archie had been interested in the producer, although I still don't know why. Care to tell me?"

"Not at the moment, sir. However, if anything transpires that is germane to the case, we will of course keep you and the *Gazette* in mind. I will turn you over to Archie," Wolfe said, hanging up.

"So I find myself stuck with you," Lon said. "Is that what is known as a consolation prize?"

"I have been called far worse," I told him. "Have the police charged Ennis with murder?"

"Not yet, but then, it's somewhat awkward to pin the tail on a donkey who's unconscious."

"Any word as to whether Ennis will pull through?"

"Nothing that we have been able to find out. Maybe you and your boss would have better luck than us in worming information out of your old pal Cramer."

"You know better than that. The inspector is hardly what one would term our 'old pal.'"

"Still, you do have something of an in with him."

I laughed. "After what has happened, I doubt that we will be hearing much if anything from the inspector about the death of Roy Breckenridge."

"Do not be too sure," Lon said.

# CHAPTER 19

In my years working for Nero Wolfe, I have learned the meanings of many words I never knew existed when I was growing up in Chillicothe, Ohio. One of these words is *prescient*, which means, if I've got it right, "having foreknowledge of events." The reason I bring this up is because Wolfe has described Lon Cohen as "prescient" more than once.

I put aside all thoughts of the Breckenridge case the next morning, and by eleven o'clock, I had typed all the letters Wolfe had dictated the day before. I was stacking them on his desk blotter when I heard two sounds simultaneously: the whir of the elevator descending from the plant rooms and the ringing of the doorbell. I headed for the front hall just as Wolfe walked into the office.

I took one look through the one-way glass in the door and did an about-face, retracing my steps. "Inspector Cramer has come to call on us yet again," I told Wolfe as he settled into his chair.

He drew in air and exhaled loudly. "Let him in." I did and was ignored as the head of New York's homicide police went by me without a word and parked as usual in the red leather chair. I waited for him to pull out a cigar, but he did not, leaning forward and placing his hands on his knees.

"I suppose you know that one of the members of that damned Broadway show, by the name of Max Ennis, tried to kill himself in his Greenwich Village flat yesterday," Cramer said.

"I read about it in this morning's *Times*," Wolfe said. "Is Mr. Ennis alive?"

"Hanging on by a thread, so we are told."

"Was a note found?" Wolfe asked, knowing the answer.

"Of a sort. There was a piece of notepaper on a bedside table near his body with two words, printed in pencil, 'I'm sorry.' There were no fingerprints on the note except for Ennis's."

"Was there anything else of interest in his residence?"

"No, not that my men found. Certainly nothing to indicate that he had any animosity toward Breckenridge."

"Do you feel you have identified your murderer?"

The inspector did his own exhaling. "It certainly seems to look that way, on the surface," he murmured.

"You do not sound overly satisfied," Wolfe observed.

Cramer ran a hand across his ruddy brow. "Something doesn't add up, and I can't figure out why."

"I do not see how we can help you," Wolfe said.

"Maybe you can't. But Goodwin here talked to all the principals in the show, and he might have some insights."

Wolfe raised his eyebrows. "Archie was already interrogated by a man you claim is a good interviewer."

"I've read the transcript, and off the record, I thought it was very poorly done," Cramer said.

"From what was related to me, I concur," Wolfe said. "The

lieutenant needs lessons in his approach, although Archie did not distinguish himself, either."

"Thanks a heap," I said. "Just continue your conversation and pretend that I am not in the room."

"Inspector, let us back up a few steps," Wolfe said. "Is it conclusive that Mr. Breckenridge was poisoned?"

"No doubt about it; arsenic, the same thing that Ennis took. We found the stuff in his flat."

"Have you determined any motive for Mr. Ennis's apparent animus toward the producer?"

"We have interviewed everyone in the cast, along with members of the staff, and at least one person said the two were involved in a heated shouting match a week or so back."

"Indeed. Who heard this?"

"A young actress, Melissa Cartwright, who said they barked at each other in Ennis's dressing room after one of the performances. She said the door was closed, so she didn't hear any details of their argument, only the yelling, which she told us went on for some time."

"You talked to Miss Cartwright," Wolfe said, turning to me. "She said nothing about this occurrence?"

"She did not. This appears to be my day to look stupid," I said. "In my defense, bear in mind that I was supposed to be a friendly journalist working for a publication, albeit fictional, that supports and promotes stage productions. As we discussed earlier, I had to be very careful in asking my questions. I did touch lightly on possible rivalries or disagreements among the cast, but got nowhere, either with Miss Cartwright or anyone else.

"The actors themselves, of course, wanted to put the best possible light on conditions and on the performances. After all, it was to their advantage to have more people—including my so-called Canadian readers—attend the show. The bigger the audiences, the longer the run, and the larger the payday for everyone."

"Archie is correct," Wolfe said. "In trying to ferret out information, he was put in an untenable position because of his role as a cheerleader for legitimate theater in general. I bear much of the responsibility for placing him in that position."

"Well, isn't this just ducky now," Cramer growled. "The man of action here is reduced to asking softball questions while trying to dig up information about supposedly strange and possibly nefarious goings-on at a high-visibility Broadway production. And the reclusive genius admits to an error in judgment in the handling of the investigation. Whatever is happening to the world?"

"If you are finished flagellating us," Wolfe said, "I have an obvious question: Why are you not convinced that Mr. Ennis is the murderer?"

"On at least one occasion, I have heard you say that you are not a big fan of coincidences," Cramer said. "You and I don't see eye-to-eye on a lot of things, but on this, we happen to agree. Something seems just too pat about what's happened, including the use of the same poison twice. It seems to me that Ennis is trying awfully hard to tell us he is the killer. It makes me wonder if he was the author of those three notes found in Breckenridge's co-op."

"Was there any similarity between that trio of notes and the one Mr. Ennis left at his home?" Wolfe asked.

"They all were printed," Cramer said, "although Ennis's 'I'm sorry' note was in pencil, the others in pen. And the penned messages were all in capital letters. They either were not printed by the same person, or that individual—if it was Ennis—worked to make it appear like it was the work of two people. We showed all four messages to a handwriting expert we have used in the past, and he just threw up his hands. 'Impossible to tell!' he said. 'Absolutely impossible to tell with printing. If I were to guess— and a guess is all it would be—I would say the so-called suicide note was written by a different person than the others, but then, he may have been trying to vary his printing intentionally.'"

Wolfe turned again to me. "At the risk of making you repeat yourself, give us your impressions of your meeting with Mr. Ennis."

Even though I had told all of it to Wolfe before, I knew this was for Cramer's benefit, so I unloaded again. "The first thing that hit me about Ennis was his lousy physical condition. Sure, he is overweight, that's a given, but onstage, he seemed to handle it well. When I talked to him in his dressing room, though, he complained about his health, told me he felt like hell most of the time.

"He said he was happy that Breckenridge had cast him in this play, but when I asked him if they were old friends, he did not answer directly, just said, 'We go back a long way.' He also told me that being in the production was a good experience, although he clearly had little use for Ashley Williston. Ennis conceded that she had talent, but added that she could be a bitch. He had been in the cast of a show with her some years back and said that if they had ever been on the stage at the same time—they hadn't—he 'might have done something violent.'"

Wolfe turned to Cramer. "I assume you or one of your men interviewed Ennis."

"I did myself," he growled, glaring at Wolfe and then at me, as if daring us to contradict him. "He was a long way from being healthy, all right. He seemed pretty broken up over Breckenridge, but then, he might have been putting on an act. After all, that's what the guy gets paid to do."

"But you do not think he is the killer," Wolfe stated.

"I know it seems like I'm making things hard on myself and on the department as a whole," Cramer said, waving a hand. "After all, there is an easy and believable way to end this investigation: We just state that we feel Ennis killed Breckenridge and then tried to do himself in. It makes perfect sense."

"But not to you," Wolfe remarked. "Did your interviews with the others in the cast and crew suggest another option?"

"Not really. Every one of them seemed genuinely fond of Breckenridge, or they at least respected him. I will say, though, that the Williston dame is one piece of goods. Arrogant, officious, enamored of herself. She acted as if she was surprised that we even talked to her. 'Surely you cannot suspect *me*?' the woman said at least three times. 'I had only the highest regard for dear Roy, who was a prince, an absolute prince. You must find the individual who committed this dastardly deed.'"

"She actually used 'dastardly deed'?" I said.

Cramer nodded glumly. "I didn't know whether to laugh or cry."

"Did you learn anything of substance from one or more of the others?" Wolfe asked.

"Not really. Most of them seemed like they were in shock."

"It appears likely that Mr. Breckenridge's cola drink was poisoned by someone entering that backstage booth from which he watched the performances. Was anyone seen entering the booth?"

"We asked, and nobody seemed to notice," Cramer said. "What about you, Goodwin? You were back there when he died."

"I was concentrating on the action onstage," I said. "Once more, I seem to have struck out."

Wolfe ignored my comment. "The papers have written that the show will not be performed for at least the next few days to honor Mr. Breckenridge. Do you have any other information?"

"No, although the cast and crew seemed more concerned

about their loss of income than about Breckenridge's death. And now, if the show is to be continued, it will need a replacement for Ennis. Say, why are you still so damned interested, Wolfe? You don't have a client anymore."

"But I do, Inspector. Someone else has stepped forward."

"I might have known. So that's why you've been pumping me for information. Who's paying you?"

"No, sir, that is not a topic under discussion here. But for your information, I am receiving no money for my services."

"Hah! That will be the day. So you are going to continue to pursue an investigation?" Cramer asked with a scowl.

"As I assume you are, sir."

"Nuts! Everybody—the mayor, the governor, the artistic community, the do-gooder civic groups, and, of course, the press—wants a killer, and they all want him—or possibly her—immediately, if not sooner. Just out of curiosity, what makes you think it isn't Ennis?"

"You know far more than I about the intricacies of the case at this point, given all your resources, and you do not appear to be comfortable with Mr. Ennis as the killer. If you are not satisfied, why should I be?"

That seemed to stump Cramer, who rose and swore. "I know one thing: I have been in this job too damned long," he muttered, slapping on his battered fedora, marching out of the office without another word, and heading down the hall in the direction of the front door. After he left the brownstone, I watched as he slowly descended the front steps in his heavy-footed gait and climbed into the backseat of a dark, unmarked car that was idling at the curb.

I returned to the office, where Wolfe sat with his eyes closed and his hands steepled. "I thought the inspector was unusually candid today," I told him.

"Mr. Cramer is conflicted, and with reason, Archie. As he pointed out, it would be easy for him to make a case for Mr. Ennis as the murderer, but his conscience will not let him do so."

"Okay, that's his problem, and I don't envy him. After all, this is what he gets paid for. But what about us?"

Wolfe eyed the book on his desk blotter, obviously wanting to return to it, but he knew I was not about to let up on him until he made a decision. "Telephone Saul and see if he is able to come here this afternoon," he said, picking up his book, *Silent Spring* by Rachel Carson.

# CHAPTER 20

Over the years, many people have underestimated Saul Panzer, to their regret. He does not present an impressive facade: five feet seven, 140 pounds, and with a mug that always needs a shave and is about two-thirds nose. He usually wears a well-worn brown or gray suit and a flat cap. No fashion plate, that one.

So much for statistics and appearance. Now on to the important stuff. Saul is simply the smartest and best freelance operative west of the Atlantic Ocean, and one Wolfe uses often. He can hold a tail better than any bloodhound, and his deep-set gray eyes never forget a face or any other detail. To Wolfe, the man can do no wrong, and more than once, he has said he trusts Saul "further than might be thought credible." I agree, and I also concede, based on long and painful experience, that he is the best poker player I have ever come across.

Saul sat in the red leather chair that afternoon, sipping

coffee. "You have read about the death of Roy Breckenridge," Wolfe said.

"Yeah, heckuva thing. Somebody spiked his Coke with arsenic."

"Archie and I had been hired by Mr. Breckenridge to investigate what he felt were troubling aspects of the play he was producing."

"Lovin' babe!" Saul said. That is the closest he ever comes to swearing. "So . . . that must be why the sketch of that Canadian 'mystery man' in the *Daily News* bore something of a resemblance to Archie. I thought about it briefly, and then I figured what the heck, these police sketches could be of almost anyone. Besides, at the time, I didn't know about your connection with the play."

"Knowing you read each New York paper every day, I assumed you would have seen that sketch and noted the resemblance," Wolfe said, his cheeks creased in what counts as a smile for him. "Let me explain the situation." He then gave Saul a concise summary of the events from Breckenridge's visit to us up until the present.

"So let me get this straight. Cramer knows Archie masqueraded as Alan MacGregor, but he hasn't said anything about it publicly, and Lon knows something funny is going on, but he isn't quite sure what it is," Saul said.

"That is about the sum of it," I said. "Quite a mess, huh?"

"Where do I fit in all this?" Saul asked Wolfe.

"I have been engaged by Lewis Hewitt, a longtime acquaintance of mine who also was a friend of Mr. Breckenridge and an investor in *Death at Cresthaven*, to identify Mr. Breckenridge's killer. I am going to ask Mr. Hewitt to request that each member of the show's cast, along with the stage manager, come here individually for conversations with me. Mr. Hewitt will be present for these interviews, and I would also like you to be here as my assistant, Saul.

"This is normally Archie's function, of course," Wolfe continued. "However, given his role as the ersatz Canadian magazine writer, he would be a distraction, to say nothing of the animosity he would likely generate among these individuals when they discover they have been gulled. He will, however, watch each of the proceedings from the alcove."

"As I suggested earlier, when you and Cramer were discussing me, just pretend I am not in the room," I said. "Or, if you would rather, I could go to the kitchen and get under Fritz's skin so you can say anything about yours truly that comes to mind."

"Do you find this assignment acceptable to you?" Wolfe asked Saul.

"Absolutely," said Saul, who has been known to drop everything else on his plate to work for Wolfe. These two have a mutual admiration society.

"Excellent. I will talk to Mr. Hewitt and make arrangements for him to inform the members of the production to come to the brownstone, preferably within a day or so."

"Do you think they all will agree to that?" Saul asked.

"I believe they will if Mr. Hewitt insists upon it. After all, he is a heavy investor in the play and now has assumed the de facto production role."

"Right now, I would like Archie to give me a rundown on each of them," Saul said, turning to me. "I need all the help I can get."

"I will leave you both," Wolfe said, rising and walking out of the office, destination: the plant rooms.

"So you have got a real treat in store for you," I told Saul. For the next half hour, I gave him my thoughts on everyone in the cast, along with Hollis Sperry. He scribbled a few notes, but not many. Like me, he retains what he hears.

"I realize that you had to tread lightly when talking to these people because of the role you got stuck playing, but Mr. Wolfe will have no such limitations," Saul said. "Think there might be some fireworks?"

"If so, some of them likely will come from Ashley Williston, she of the hyperactive ego. The woman acted shocked that Cramer would dare to even question her, and knowing him, I am sure he went easy. Just think how she is going to react when Wolfe bores in on her."

"Given his general attitude about women, and overbearing ones in particular, I would say such will be likely," Saul agreed. "Well, you'll get to watch any fireworks yourself, albeit from offstage."

He was referring to Wolfe's comment that I would be observing the events from the "alcove." That nook, at the end of the hall next to the kitchen, contains a peephole that allows one to view the office without detection. The peephole is camouflaged within a painting of a waterfall that hangs on one wall, and it has been put to use numerous times over the years by Wolfe, me, and in a few cases, a client. No visitor to the office has ever spotted it.

"The next time I see you, you won't see me," I told Saul.

"Are you saying you'll have my back?"

"Actually, from my vantage point, I'll have your profile, and quite a profile it is."

"No nose jokes," Saul cracked, "or I will be forced to remind you about that dandy pot in our game last Thursday night, when you kept raising me because you thought I was beaten by your small straight—make that a *very* small straight."

"Okay, I stand chagrined. I also stand light in the wallet, thanks in large part to those hot hands you kept having. What a run of luck that was."

"May I remind you that it is not luck, but rather, skill—skill honed over long years of studying the faces and habits of my fellow combatants. For instance, whenever you have what you think is a winning hand, you invariably . . . but no, I am not about to give away one of my many trade secrets."

"You are all heart, as I have often remarked. Whatever it is I do to telegraph my hands, I hereby resolve to stop it."

"Good luck with that, Archie," Saul said. "How about we play some gin rummy to pass the time?"

We did, and for once, I did surprisingly well. That is to say, we broke even.

# CHAPTER 21

I put Wolfe through to Lewis Hewitt later in the day, and things started to move. The next morning, Hewitt called to say he had talked to all the principals in *Cresthaven* and had gotten them to agree to come to the brownstone, although not without some resistance.

"I had one devil of a time with Ashley, which is hardly a surprise," Hewitt told me, "but after I pointed out that her absence might be interpreted as suspicious, she relented, but she did plenty of whining, and believe me, she knows how to whine. I reminded her that the sooner we get to the bottom of what happened to Roy, the sooner the play can resume."

"Ah, she can still taste that elusive Tony Award, right?"

"Yes, and now that I am in charge of the production by dint of my being its largest investor, I have no compunctions about exerting pressure on the woman in question."

"Is that what's called playing hardball?"

"You could say so, Archie. It will be fascinating to watch Ashley spar with Mr. Wolfe."

"My money's on my boss," I said. "She won't lay a glove on him."

"Do not be too sure," Hewitt said. "Ashley is one cunning lady. I think you will find she can get under Nero Wolfe's skin."

"I believe you are a fan of Rusterman's Restaurant, aren't you?"

"I certainly am; it is probably the best place in Midtown, and maybe in the whole city, for that matter. Why do you ask?"

"I propose a wager. If Wolfe gets the best of the actress, as I believe he will, you buy me dinner at Rusterman's. If Miss Williston comes out on top, anything you want to order will be my treat."

"Ah, but who decides the winner?"

"Let us stipulate that we both have to agree. And if we can't, we each will pay our own way."

"That sounds good to me. You're on," Hewitt said.

The schedule now was complete. Hollis Sperry would be Wolfe's first visitor, at nine tonight, followed by Teresa Reed at eleven thirty tomorrow morning and Steve Peters at nine that night. The others would follow over the next couple of days. Wolfe was by no means happy, and I know he wished he had taken Hewitt's suggestion that the theater people come to the brownstone en masse. But he had said, "It will be more instructive to see them separately, so they are not influenced by one another's recollections and opinions."

He was now stuck with his plan, which meant that at least portions of several days would be disrupted, interfering with his reading but not, thank heavens, with his twice-daily séances with the orchids up on the roof.

Five minutes before Sperry was scheduled to arrive, Lewis Hewitt settled in with a scotch and soda on one of the yellow chairs in the office. Wolfe was in the kitchen planning the next day's meals with Fritz, and Saul was in the front hall, preparing to play doorman. I was in the alcove, peering into the office. Because Wolfe and I are both five feet eleven, we had the peephole made to suit us, and on the occasions when shorter individuals have needed to use it—including two female clients who helped identify murderers—they have stood on a stool. People taller than Wolfe and me who need to use the peephole . . . well, they just have to slouch a little.

I heard the doorbell, and within a minute, Saul entered the room with Sperry, who was wearing a dark suit and who exchanged pleasantries with Hewitt before taking the red leather chair while Saul sat at my desk as if he belonged there.

"I am supposed to meet with Nero Wolfe, but frankly, I do not see the point of it," Sperry grouched. "I have been interviewed twice by the cops, and they know everything that I know about what happened. I am wrung dry. You can't get blood out of a turnip."

"I appreciate your frustration, Hollis," Hewitt said. "But so far, and with all due respect to them, the police do not appear to be making much progress. Mr. Wolfe, who happens to be an old friend of mine, has uncanny abilities to discover the truth in cases that seem beyond the abilities of others."

Sperry did not look convinced and wore a frown when Wolfe entered the room, detoured around his desk, sat, and considered his guest. "Good evening, sir, and thank you for coming. I assume you already have met my colleague Mr. Panzer."

"Yes, I have, but I'm not really sure why I am here. I don't see how I can be of any help," the stage manager said, fidgeting in his chair.

"We shall get to that," Wolfe said. "But first, will you have something to drink? As you can see, Mr. Hewitt already has been served, and I am having beer."

"Thanks, but—oh, why the hell not? If you don't mind, I'll have a scotch on the rocks." Wolfe gestured to Saul, who went to the serving cart against the wall and poured the scotch, handing it to Sperry, who clearly was uncomfortable. I noticed a tic on the right side of his face, one I hadn't seen before.

"As to why you are here," Wolfe said after Sperry had sampled his drink and nodded in approval, "I have been engaged by Mr. Hewitt to determine the cause of Roy Breckenridge's death, and in addition to you, I am going to be speaking to all the cast members."

"Even after Max's suicide attempt, does that mean that all of us are suspects? By the way, do you know how Max is faring?"

"Max, as far as I know, although still in a coma, is holding his own. As for you being suspects, I cannot speak for the police department, nor would I presume to do so. However, is it not fair to say each of you had the opportunity to dispatch Mr. Breckenridge?"

"Well, obviously, we all were in the theater when he died, if that's your point," Sperry huffed.

"Do you think Mr. Ennis had a motive for murdering the producer?"

"If he did, I'm surely not aware of what it was," Sperry said. "As far as I could tell, they seemed to get along quite well."

"Were you aware of Mr. Breckenridge's penchant for Coca-Cola?"

"Of course, and so, probably, was everybody else connected with the show, including the crew. He drank the stuff by the gallon. Always had. He claimed it gave him the jolt he needed."

"You had known him for a long time?" Saul asked, giving Wolfe a chance to drink his beer.

"I had, probably twenty-five years or close to that. He always said I was his favorite stage manager, probably because I put up with his obsession for control. After all, Roy liked to function as both producer and director, and a lot of the time, he functioned in effect as the stage manager as well."

"Did you find that discomfiting?" Wolfe asked.

"Yes and no. I don't believe in false modesty, and I happen to be very good at what I do. I have been stage-managing on Broadway for more than half my life, and it's irritating when somebody tries to tell me how to do my job, even someone as successful as Roy. To his credit, though, when I pushed back against some of his decrees—and that's what I called them, *decrees*—he would back off and allow as to how I was correct."

"Did he have any enemies you were aware of?"

"I can't imagine anyone involved in *Death at Cresthaven*. Oh, of course Ashley Williston could be hard to get along with, always wanting to change her lines or alter some stage direction. During rehearsals, both Roy and I would cringe whenever she began with 'I think this scene would work better if . . .' One or the other of us frequently had to rein her in and remind her that we don't mess with the playwright's work. It seems incredible that someone with all her experience would suggest some of the things she did."

"Did the actress ever threaten Mr. Breckenridge?"

"Even Ashley, as arrogant and full of herself as she is, knew better than to go up against Roy too often. He was not a vindictive man by nature, but if someone got on the wrong side of him, he could be tough to deal with, very tough."

"Could he, and would he, blackball someone?" Saul asked.

I could see the tic in Sperry's face again, and he struggled to get comfortable.

"If so, I never heard about it, at least not in a formal sense," he replied. "However, although I was not involved in the particular production, I do know of one case where an actor with a fondness for the bottle showed up for rehearsals loaded two days in a row, and Roy blew his top. He threw the guy off the cast and said, 'You will never work for me again!' That comment got around town fast, and to my knowledge, it pretty well finished the schmo's career, at least in big-time productions. Last I knew, and that was some time back, he was reduced to working in summer stock and small regional theaters."

"You have mentioned frustrations with Miss Williston," Wolfe said. "Did Mr. Breckenridge find any others in this cast difficult to work with?"

"Not at all. Every one of them, even the young ones, are very professional and even-tempered. The only problems any of them had that I was aware of were with Ashley and her dominating personality. I've also heard that she showed a, shall we say . . . *nonprofessional* interest in Steve Peters, who, as you probably know, is at least a generation younger than she."

"Was that interest reciprocated?" Wolfe asked.

"It was not, which led to some tension, as you can imagine. The two of you have been asking a lot of questions," Sperry said. "Now I have one for you: Has anything been heard of that mysterious Canadian writer, MacGregor, who hung around the set and interviewed all of us, supposedly for a magazine article? I've read in the papers that the cursed magazine doesn't even exist, and that even the police don't seem to know who this character is."

"We cannot help you there, sir," Wolfe said. "Did he seem genuine to you?"

Sperry shrugged. "I suppose so. I have not been interviewed all that often in the past, stage managers rarely are, so I don't have anyone to compare him with. Mine is not exactly what you would refer to as a glamour job, nor is it a popular job. Actors hate being scolded, and my role entails plenty of scolding."

"I would like to return to your comment about Ashley Williston and Steve Peters. Was Mr. Breckenridge cognizant of the tension between them?"

"Of course he was; Roy doesn't—didn't—miss much."

"Such has been said of him, which brings me to a salient point: I am told he recently expressed concern about a malaise that he felt permeated the atmosphere at the theater."

Sperry jerked upright. "Huh! Where did you hear that?"

"The source is immaterial. You may have known Mr. Breckenridge longer than anyone else involved in the play, with the possible exception of Mr. Ennis. Are you saying he never appeared to show concern over what he viewed as problems with the production or its participants?"

"If something was bothering Roy, he didn't let it show, at least not around me," Sperry said. "Going back to the business with Ashley and Peters, he did say to me, 'That woman is up to her old tricks again.'"

"Meaning?"

"Meaning Ashley has always had an eye—and more than an eye, really—for younger men, particularly good-looking ones, and Mr. Peters definitely falls into those categories."

"Did Mr. Breckenridge take any action to stifle Miss Williston's predilection?"

"If so, he did not tell me, although in the last few days, she didn't seem to be flirting with Peters like she had before, so it's possible Roy said something to her."

Wolfe drank beer and set his glass down. "Do you believe Mr. Ennis attempted suicide?"

"It sure seems that way to me," Sperry replied, drumming his fingers on the arm of the chair.

"Can you suggest a reason?"

"As you might know, Max is not in very good shape, to say the least. Hell, he has to be at least eighty, maybe even a little more. When he was onstage, he managed to look okay, but I knew how much effort that was taking for him—and taking out of him. Between acts and at the end of a performance, he sagged and seemed like he aged ten years. Maybe it all finally got to the guy."

"Did he complain about being in pain?"

"I never heard any gripes out of Max, but then, he is old school, what they refer to as a real trouper."

"Is he well liked by the others in the cast?"

"It seems like it to me. He is something of a father figure, you could say, at least for the younger actors, and also for the understudies. Several times, I noticed him huddled with either Steve or Melissa, apparently giving them encouragement or sympathy, maybe both, after a performance. He is a nice contrast to Ashley, who, obviously, is far from the nurturing type. She is much too busy thinking about her career and her desire for a Tony to worry about anyone or anything else."

"Hardly a character reference," Wolfe said dryly.

"I am sure you would get a similar response from dozens of others on Broadway who have come in contact with her over the years."

"How did she and Mr. Ennis get along?"

Sperry snorted, eyeing his empty glass. "They were civil to each other, but hardly convivial. It was obvious to me that Max felt she had an exalted opinion of herself, while she tended to give him a wide berth. She knew she couldn't bully him. He had too much stature in the business."

"Did either of them ever criticize the other to you?" Saul asked.

Sperry waved the comment away. "Nah, they both were smart enough to know it wouldn't accomplish a darned thing. For what it's worth, I've got a reputation of not having much tolerance for whiners and backbiters, of which there are plenty in our little world. The same was true of Roy. Cast members were expected to be professional, to show up well prepared for rehearsals and performances, and to not make themselves look good at the expense of others. Sorry if that sounds like a sermon, but that is how both Roy and I ran a show. I told you before that we didn't always agree on everything, and that his need for total control sometimes frustrated me, but there was nobody else I would rather work for."

"It seems apparent he also valued you highly," Wolfe said.

Sperry nodded curtly. "All I can say is that I was his stage manager on six . . . no, make that seven productions. Look, I really don't know what else I can tell you," he said, getting to his feet.

"I just hope that you, or the cops, or somebody, finds out who did this." He turned to Hewitt. "I know you are more or less in charge of the production now, which is just fine with me. Any idea when, or if, we are going to resume?"

"That is hard to say right now, Hollis. It seems unlikely there will be any more performances until everything gets resolved. We will need a new director as well as a replacement for Max. All of which means that before the show can start up again, there will have to be another whole batch of rehearsals."

"I know that, of course," the stage manager said with a grimace. "A lot of people involved in *Cresthaven*—cast, crew, backers—would love to get it back on the stage, most of all Ashley, who sees her chance at winning that Tony about to go down the drain." Sperry shook his head and walked out of the office without a good-bye, with Saul following him down the hall to the front door.

I emerged from hiding and sat in my desk chair as Saul was returning. "Well, what's the consensus?" I asked.

"You like to give odds, Archie," Saul said. "I make it three to two that Sperry's clean."

"I cannot imagine him as a killer," Hewitt said. "But then, I frankly can't imagine any of them committing murder, so I am a poor one to judge. Chalk it up to my naïveté."

"After standing at that peephole for however long it was, I am just happy to be sitting down," I put in. "But I will agree with Saul that the odds are at least three to two that the stage manager is in the clear, although he did seem nervous."

"You're right about that," Saul said. "He seemed awfully antsy, but then, he was being subjected to an inquisition of sorts, which would make almost anyone nervous."

Wolfe pursed his lips. "Mr. Sperry appears to be earnest and dedicated, although those attributes do not necessarily absolve him. I prefer to withhold judgment until we meet with the others."

"Do you honestly think *Death at Cresthaven* will ever be performed again?" I asked Hewitt.

"I would like to think so, but in addition to being naive, I also am a realist, Archie. Getting a replacement for Max is possible, but finding a new director, that is a good deal more difficult, especially with Ashley in the cast. Heaven knows when we could be ready to perform again. And if Max Ennis should die, it would seem grossly insensitive to even contemplate continuing with the production anytime in the near future."

"Yeah, two deaths are a lot to overcome all right. Any late word on Ennis's condition?"

"As of about noon today, there was no change. He is still in a coma, although according to the doctor I spoke with on the telephone, his vital signs were strong."

"Look on the bright side," I told Wolfe. "Tomorrow morning, you will have the pleasure of spending some time with Teresa Reed, she of the keen eye and the sharp tongue."

Wolfe glowered but said nothing. He has little use for women in the brownstone, particularly acerbic ones, and our next visitor was nothing if not acerbic.

# CHAPTER 22

The next morning, Lewis Hewitt and Saul arrived at the brownstone at eleven, and the three of us sat in the office with coffee while Wolfe, fresh from his morning session playing up in the plant rooms, repaired to the kitchen, presumably to discuss the lunch menu with Fritz.

Hewitt turned to me. "Do you think all these interviews are likely to accomplish anything?"

"You should pose that question to Wolfe. He has his ways, and as long as I have worked with the man, I still don't always understand his approach. But then, he is a genius."

Saul nodded. "I agree. I have known Mr. Wolfe almost as long as Archie has, and I've seen him pull more rabbits out of hats than the Great Blackstone, magician supreme."

"It will be interesting to see what kind of magic he can pull off with Teresa Reed," I said. "Based on the single conversation I had with her, it wouldn't surprise me if my boss got so frustrated, he got up and walked out of the office. I have seen that happen before, more than once."

Hewitt chuckled. "She is something of a harpy, no question. She almost always plays acid-tongued characters, which is no accident. The difference between her stage persona and the real Teresa is almost imperceptible. The woman has taken sarcasm to new levels, and she has driven directors and stage managers to distraction, although I will say this for her: She is smart as well as being a fine actress, and she does not suffer fools gladly."

"How did she get along with Breckenridge and Sperry?" Saul asked.

"Actually pretty well, from what I've been able to learn as something of an outsider," Hewitt said. "Roy told me once some weeks back that she could be difficult, although nothing like Ashley. 'When Teresa has a beef, there is usually a pretty good reason,' he said. And I would agree with that. She takes a fierce pride in her professionalism."

"This should be interesting," Saul said as the doorbell rang. He went down the hall to greet the interviewee while I headed for the alcove and its peephole.

Teresa Reed marched into the office like an army officer about to review the troops, but when she saw Hewitt, she stopped short. "I know that you asked me to be here, but I did not realize you would be present. Why is that?" she demanded.

"Mr. Wolfe asked me to sit in on the conversations with members of the cast," he replied amiably. "After all, as you know, this is, for all intents and purposes, my production now."

"Huh! After what's happened, is there even going to be a production?" she demanded, taking the red leather chair Hewitt was offering. "And where is this Nero Wolfe person that I am supposed to see? This so-called miracle worker?"

"Good morning, madam," Wolfe said as he strode into the

room and settled into the chair behind his desk. "Would you like something to drink, coffee perhaps? I am having beer."

"Beer in the morning? How very quaint. Do you do that to burnish your reputation as being some sort of an eccentric?"

"I do it because I happen to like beer. Do you find such to be offensive?"

"Offensive, no; posturing, perhaps; unhealthy, almost surely. But it is, of course, your business and no one else's."

"Thank you for acknowledging that. Now I would like to—"

"Before we go any further, what is the latest word on poor Max?"

"He is hanging on," Hewitt told Teresa. "Still in a coma, however."

"And one more thing," she said, "what about that MacGregor fraud who interviewed all of us? Why haven't the police found him? I knew there was something phony about the man from the first. A reporter working for an arts magazine in Canada—hah!"

Wolfe drew in a bushel of air and exhaled slowly. "Madam, as far as I know, Mr. MacGregor has not been located by the police. He—"

"Speaking of the police, are they doing anything to find Breckenridge's killer? Or have they turned the case over to you?"

"Enough!" Wolfe roared, slapping his palm down on the desk.

Teresa Reed's thin rear end lifted off the chair in reaction to the gunshot-like sound, and I stifled a laugh. "I did not realize that you find it necessary to resort to shouting," she said in a voice that carried the slightest quaver.

"Only when it is necessary to stop a barrage of interruptions. It is my understanding you came here to answer questions, not to ask them."

"Well, excuse me, Mr. Nero Wolfe. Go ahead and ask whatever you want to," she snapped.

"Thank you, I shall. Do you have reason to believe someone wished Mr. Breckenridge ill?"

"I do not. Granted, he wasn't always the most likable person in the room, but he was an effective leader, good at what he did, in fact, very good."

"What made him unlikable?"

Teresa squirmed in her chair. "Roy could be impatient with people to the point of rudeness. I saw this many times during rehearsals. Also, he had what I felt was an inordinate fondness for the ladies."

"Including those with whom he worked?"

"I did not say that! But he had a . . . well, a reputation."

"To what degree is that hearsay?"

"*Hearsay*—I assume that's a fancy word for *gossip*."

"To be accurate, it is synonymous with *rumor*," Wolfe said.

"Same thing, as far as I'm concerned," Teresa said, readjusting herself in her chair, aiming her hawklike nose at Wolfe and swallowing hard. "I have heard enough stories about him, and from reputable sources, to believe there is truth to it."

"But I take it you have no specifics?"

She sniffed. "Well . . . no."

"I have been led to believe there was a degree of tension among members of the cast. Did you find this to be so?"

"Well, any cast that has Ashley Williston in it is bound to have some tension. And that, sir, does not happen to be hearsay. I have seen it firsthand in *Death at Cresthaven* and also heard it from actor friends of mine who were in the cast with her in two other plays. She always feels she knows more than anyone else involved in a staging, whether it is a cast member, the makeup staff, the director, the stage manager, or even the producer, for God's sake."

"How would you describe her relationship with Mr. Breckenridge?" Saul asked.

"I assume you mean *professional* relationship?"

"Is there any other kind?"

"Not as far as I am aware, lest you think me a rumormonger."

"No one is suggesting such, madam," Wolfe said.

"Well, thank you for *that*, anyway," she said, squirming. "As to their relationship, I would describe it as strained at best. Ashley always had a better idea—when to make her entry, where to sit or stand, how to react to someone else's lines. To hear her go on, one would think she was the playwright, director, and stage manager, all rolled into one."

"Was Mr. Breckenridge able to corral her?" Wolfe asked.

"Good choice of a verb," she said with a nod. "She could be like a bucking bronco. But if I can continue the analogy, Roy never got unhorsed. He could be just as stubborn as Ashley, maybe even more so."

"How did Miss Williston react to being overruled?"

"Oh, she pouted of course, as one would expect, but she was smart enough to know when to quit fighting Roy. After all, Ashley saw this as probably her last chance to win a Tony, as I am sure you have heard already. Personally, I do not think she would have gotten the award anyway, not with the raves that Marshall woman is getting in the long-running drama playing over at the Winter Garden."

"Were there other conflicts among the cast?"

Teresa Reed screwed up her face. "I know that I am going to sound like I have it in for Ashley, but you asked. She seemed to think she could charm young Steve Peters. During rehearsals, she was forever flirting with him. Old enough to be his mother! It was absolutely disgusting."

Wolfe exhaled. "How did Mr. Peters react to her coquetry?"

"How do you think?" she snapped. "Here the poor guy was trying to make his name in a well-publicized Broadway production, and he didn't know how to handle her aggression. He was somewhat in awe of Ashley and her semidistinguished career, and the last thing he wanted was to alienate her. I felt sorry for the guy, as much as I ever feel sorry for anybody who gets into this crazy business. After all, as actors, we are supposed to deal with tough challenges, both onstage and off."

"Did either Mr. Breckenridge or Mr. Sperry intercede in the one-sided dalliance?"

Teresa sneered. "They both pretended to ignore it, don't ask me why. Maybe they felt they already had enough trouble with Queen Ashley without wading into this predicament."

"Did the situation resolve itself?" Wolfe asked.

"In a sense, yes. As far as I could discern, Peters did not return her interest, although he continued to be deferential toward her. One other thing . . ."

"Yes?"

"It seemed to me that that Melissa Cartwright had an active interest in Peters herself. One could see that she was far from pleased with Ashley's antics toward him."

"Did Mr. Peters return the young woman's interest?"

"Hard to tell," Teresa said. "He is a difficult one to read. Even when Ashley was vamping him—and not doing a very good job of it, if you ask me—whatever revulsion he may have felt, he kept well hidden. If I were to guess, though, I would say he was drawn to Melissa. Have you met her?"

"Not yet," Wolfe said.

"She is an attractive young woman, no question about that."

"Is it unusual to have this much intrigue, particularly of an amorous nature, in a Broadway show?" Saul asked.

The character actress nodded. "I would say so. Oh, there have been a few liaisons here and there in plays I've been involved with, but the goings-on during *Cresthaven* have seemed somewhat more intense."

"Mr. Breckenridge had said he felt a sense of unease was pervading the production," Wolfe said. "Do you feel that may have been because of these relationships?"

"Of course I have no way of knowing that—how could I?" Teresa said. "I try to mind my own business. Roy may have been referring to Ashley's resentment of Brad Lester."

"What caused this resentment on her part?" Wolfe asked.

"Her Highness had heard or read somewhere, maybe in *Variety*, that Lester had been brought into the cast for box-office appeal, given his star status in films. Ashley has long claimed to have no respect whatever for Hollywood, and what galled her most—I know this because she told me—is that Lester's name came before hers on the theater marquee and in the playbill."

"Did this resentment manifest itself in the production?"

"It was particularly evident in rehearsals, where she complained that Lester was pausing too long to deliver his lines after she had spoken, or that, on at least one occasion, he came onstage too quickly."

"Was she justified in these complaints?" Saul asked.

"She definitely was not," Teresa said, waving her hand dismissively. "It was an attempt, and a very transparent one, to make Lester look bad, but it did not work, because Roy jumped in and defended him, saying things like 'No, I think his timing was perfect.' Ashley was furious, but then, what could she do? She had been caught out, she knew it, and she knew that Roy knew it. There was no more of that nonsense for the rest of the rehearsals, or when the run began. But she was still bitter, and offstage she has been cool to Lester to the point of iciness."

"How has Mr. Lester behaved toward her?"

"As if nothing had ever happened, at least as far as I was able to tell. He is both a first-rate actor and a gentleman. Ashley could take lessons from him on how to behave with class."

"It would appear that Miss Williston is the source of much of the discord surrounding the production," Wolfe said.

"Hah! That is putting it mildly, Mr. Genius," Teresa said.

Wolfe ignored the dig. "Let us turn to the subject of Mr. Ennis; do you have any thoughts as to why he would try to do away with himself?"

"If you have done your homework, as you should, you are aware that Max was failing. While onstage, he did a damned good job of hiding his ailments, but all of us knew how much pain he always seemed to be in. He did not do a lot of complaining, though, because he is a true professional."

"Do you feel there is a correlation between Mr. Breckenridge's apparent murder and Mr. Ennis's suicide attempt?"

"I hope you are not suggesting that Max poisoned Roy. The idea is absolutely preposterous, and I am amazed you would come up with it."

"I make no such suggestion, madam. Were you or anyone else in the company surprised by Mr. Ennis's action?"

"I think it is fair to say we all were shocked, terribly shocked."

"How would you describe the relationship between the men?"

Teresa sniffed again, as if insulted by the question. I wondered how long before she would get up and leave in a huff. "Amiable, and why wouldn't it be?" she answered. "They had worked together in the past, and they had respect for each other. It seems to me that you are going out on a limb to find trouble where none exists. If I were you, I would concentrate on locating that MacGregor individual—if that is really the man's name."

"I appreciate your suggestion," Wolfe said in a tone that indicated no such appreciation. "Is there anything else you care to add?"

"Only that I hope you begin to make some progress. You certainly haven't made any yet."

"Good day, madam," Wolfe said, rising and walking out of the office.

"Talk about being rude," Teresa grumped, looking first at Hewitt and then at Saul. "Does he always behave like that, or do I bring out the worst in people, as has been said about me?"

"Mr. Wolfe tends to be brusque," Hewitt said.

"Oh, is that what you call it, brusque? I would have said boorish. Well, I have spent quite enough time here, thank you very much," she said, getting to her feet and marching out much the same way as she marched in. Saul followed her to the door as I left my post at the peephole and went to the office.

"She is quite the character, isn't she?" Hewitt said as I sat.

"I'm not sure that is the word Wolfe would use, but she hasn't exactly mellowed with age, has she?"

"What a number she is!" Saul said, entering the office and shaking his head. "As she was leaving, she turned to me and said, 'How can you stand working for that oversize egomaniac? I hope that you get hazard pay.'"

"How did you respond?" I asked him.

"I merely nodded and smiled at her," Saul replied. "The woman has got chutzpah, I will give her that. And she also happens to be a first-rate actress; I've seen her in at least three plays, and although she wasn't ever the lead, she got the biggest applause at the curtain in two of them, with good reason."

"You are quite the man about town, aren't you?"

"Hey, Archie, I like to get around. With you, it's dancing with

Lily Rowan at the Churchill or going to the Rangers games; with me, it's poker and Broadway shows."

"Oh, it is poker with me, too," I replied, "except you mostly win while I mostly lose."

"Whaddya mean, 'mostly win'? I almost *always* win."

"Don't rub it in. You'll give Mr. Hewitt the wrong idea, and he might invite me to one of his games since I'm such an easy mark."

"Don't worry about that, Archie," Hewitt said, laughing. "I don't play poker, and if I did, I am sure Mr. Panzer would relieve me of my money, too. What do you two think of Teresa Reed as a possible suspect?"

"She certainly is nervy enough to pull off a killing," Saul said. "And although she says she respected his abilities, she wasn't overly fond of Breckenridge, as she made clear. But where's the motive? What do you think, Archie?"

"I agree with Saul on all counts. Based on my earlier interviews with the cast and watching today's performance, she is probably the smartest person in the show, with the possible exception of Max Ennis. I realize she's caustic to the point of distraction, although she is also a quick study. But a murderer? I vote probably not, although I'm not prepared to give odds. And as you have just seen in her encounter with my boss, she is not easily intimidated."

"I will add an amen!" Hewitt replied. "I'm not sure I've ever heard anyone speak to Mr. Wolfe like that before. Although he did finally shut her up after she'd been interrupting him."

"Yeah, I have to say I liked seeing the look on her face when he slapped his palm down. For him, that is an act of violence," I said.

"Say, I've forgotten, who's next on our list, and when?" Hewitt asked.

"It is young Steve Peters," I said. "And he will be joining us at nine tonight. Or, more precisely, he will be joining the two of you and Mr. Wolfe. You know where I will be."

# CHAPTER 23

Both Saul and Lewis Hewitt joined us at dinner, where Wolfe held forth on why the Wright Brothers had been so successful in the development of their airplanes as we consumed Fritz's superb casserole of lamb cutlets with gammon and tomatoes.

"This is a rare treat for me, feasting on two of Mr. Brenner's superb meals in the space of a few days," Hewitt said. "Thank you for the invitations."

Wolfe nodded his "you are welcome" and went on talking about the Wrights, who he said "were possessed of a rare singleness of purpose that allowed them to concentrate on constructing and piloting their flying machines with a minimum of distraction."

"I was privileged to meet Orville Wright at a dinner at the Waldorf a couple of years before he died," Hewitt said. "He was a fine gentleman, and extremely modest. The man lived a long life, far longer than his brother Wilbur, and he got to see incredible progress in aviation. He was one of the great Americans of the twentieth century." The conversation morphed into a wide-ranging discussion of the airlines today and their effect upon global travel.

After dinner, we moved to the office for coffee, and Wolfe turned to me. "You will not be present to talk to Mr. Peters, but if you were, what would you want to learn, now no longer fettered by playing the role of a friendly magazine writer?"

"I would start by asking him to describe his relationship to Ashley Williston."

"Don't you think that would rattle him to the point of clamming up and withdrawing into a shell?" Hewitt asked.

"Maybe, but Peters is a big boy, isn't he? Never mind his tender age, after all, this is a murder case. When I did my interviewing, I had to pussyfoot around, being careful not to make anybody suspicious. Now, we've got one murder and a possible suicide—unless somebody here thinks maybe there was a murder attempt on Ennis and that he murdered Breckenridge."

"I agree with Archie," Saul said. "I think a frontal attack is the best approach. Besides, his new producer is going to be right here in the room, and it is to Mr. Peters's benefit to do everything he can to cooperate with the investigation, unless he has reason not to. There is still a chance, however thin, that the production could be continued, and that certainly would benefit him—assuming, of course, that he is not the poisoner."

"I have no intention whatever of bullying Mr. Peters," Wolfe said. "But I am not about to handle him with kid gloves, either, and further—" He was interrupted by the doorbell. I hastened off to my post while Saul headed down the hall to play doorman yet again.

Steve Peters, dressed in a sport coat, slacks, starched white shirt, and tie, stepped into the office, looked around, and blinked. "Uh, hello, Mr. Hewitt," he said. "I think I am on time."

"You are, sir," said Wolfe. "Please be seated. Would you like something to drink? Coffee, perhaps, or beer, or something else?"

"No, nothing for me," the young actor replied, sliding uneasily into the red leather chair and looking at Wolfe in awe.

"As you know, Mr. Peters, all those intimately involved in *Death at Cresthaven* have been asked to come here at the request of Mr. Hewitt to shed whatever light they are able on the death of Roy Breckenridge and the hospitalization of Max Ennis," Wolfe said.

Peters swallowed and nodded. "I do not see how I can help. I have told the police everything I know."

"I appreciate that, and I ask your forbearance. I will try to be as expeditious as possible. In the days leading up to Mr. Breckenridge's death, did anything surrounding the play seem amiss to you, or in any way whatever out of the ordinary?"

"No sir, not really. Except now, I realize there must have been something suspicious about that Canadian magazine writer, MacGregor—at least that's what he called himself. I have read in the newspapers that the publication he claimed to represent does not even exist, and that he has disappeared. But I suppose you already know that."

"I do. Let us set the subject of Mr. MacGregor aside, at least for the moment. Did anyone connected with *Death at Cresthaven* seem to exhibit animosity toward Mr. Breckenridge?"

"Not at all, not in the least. It seemed to me that everyone respected him, as they should. He has a wonderful record on Broadway, as all of you know."

"Did anyone question his judgment as a producer or director?"

"Well . . . there were a few occasions when Ashley—Miss Williston—had questions and suggestions during rehearsals about stage direction and things of that sort."

"Did you feel she was challenging Mr. Breckenridge's authority?"

Peters shifted in his chair. No question that the young man was nervous. "I suppose her comments might be seen in that light, but then, she too has had an awfully good record."

"Did he resent her questions and suggestions?"

"I couldn't always tell, although I remember that on one occasion, he did say to her, 'Let's try this scene my way, Ashley. We simply have got to move things along.'"

"How did she react to that comment?"

"It was easy to see that she wasn't happy, but she bit her lip, and the rehearsal went on as Mr. Breckenridge had directed it."

"Miss Williston sounds like a strong personality."

"Yes, very much so."

"How did you get along with her?"

I knew Wolfe was gradually leading up to that, and I focused on Peters, who swallowed again. "She is . . . very dedicated and intense. I was fascinated watching her deliver her lines. She has got a presence about her; I don't quite have the words to describe it."

"The woman is a veteran performer, while you are a relative neophyte," Wolfe said. "How did she treat you?"

"I have no complaints whatever. Ashley is every inch a professional." I wondered how long he had practiced those lines, which came out as though they had been rehearsed.

"Did others involved in the production have different opinions about her?" Wolfe asked.

"Different opinions? I really don't know. We did not discuss other cast members among ourselves. We all were too busy rehearsing and concentrating on trying to get everything right."

"Did you ever feel she was challenging Mr. Breckenridge's authority or his judgment?"

Peters looked at Hewitt, as if seeking support. Finding none, he said to Wolfe, "Well . . . she did sometimes suggest better ways that a scene might be done."

"Did you agree with any of her suggestions?"

"Uh . . . not really. I felt Mr. Breckenridge always had good reasons for what he was doing."

"Do you have any thoughts about who might have poisoned Mr. Breckenridge?" Wolfe asked.

"None whatever, other than that MacGregor fellow. I hope they find him."

"What do you think the reason is behind Mr. Ennis's apparent suicide attempt?"

"That was terrible, just terrible," Peters said with feeling. "Is there any news on his condition?"

"Nothing has changed in the last couple of days," Hewitt put in.

"To rephrase my question: What reason would Mr. Ennis have for trying to kill himself?" Wolfe asked.

Peters shook his head. "I really don't know, unless he had recently received a bad medical diagnosis. It was clear to all of us that his health wasn't good, although he seemed somehow to get energized at the beginning of every performance. I don't know how he did it."

"It has been said that he and Mr. Breckenridge quarreled and exchanged heated words in the days before the poisoning. Do you have any knowledge of that?"

"No sir, I do not. If such a quarrel took place inside the theater, I think I would have heard something. Our dressing rooms are jammed in close together in the basement, and the walls are pretty thin, so there really is not a lot of privacy."

"Who are you closest to among the cast and the staff?"

"Mmm, nobody in particular," Peters said as I noticed beads of sweat forming on his forehead and his upper lip. "By that I don't mean to suggest we weren't friendly to one another during the production. Overall, relations were really quite cordial."

"Miss Cartwright is nearest to you in age. I would have thought you might have developed a friendship, given that everyone else in the cast is at least a generation older than the two of you."

"Oh, we are certainly friendly," he said, his face reddening. "I guess you could say we were maybe a little bit closer to each other than to anybody else. After all, we were playing an engaged couple."

"Was Miss Cartwright comfortable around each of the other members of the company?"

"Yes sir, she seemed to be, as far as I could tell. I never heard Melissa complain about anyone. But then, she does not seem like a complainer by nature. She has a very positive attitude."

"Did she have any reason to have animus toward Mr. Breckenridge? Perhaps anger over some criticism he made during rehearsals?"

"Not at all. If anything, he tended to favor her."

"In what way?"

"When he did have a criticism about her, he was much gentler than he was with any of the rest of us."

"Why was that?"

Peters turned his palms up. "Maybe he felt she was the most sensitive one in the cast and might be easily hurt by criticism. That's all I can think of."

"Did that favoritism engender resentment among others in the cast?"

"Not that I was able to detect."

Wolfe finished the beer and glared at the empty glass. "Let us now make the assumption that Max Ennis did not attempt suicide, but rather was the victim of a murder attempt."

"But that does not seem probable, does it?" Peters said, clearing his throat.

"Please, sir, humor me and indulge my assumption. Who might be most likely to want Mr. Ennis dead?"

"No one!" Peters barked, then recoiled, shocked at his own vitriol. "Everyone liked Max. How could you not? Offstage, he was like everybody's favorite uncle, as somebody else in the cast, I can't remember who, described him. I can't conceive of anyone wanting to hurt Max."

"And I gather you also cannot conceive of him wanting to do harm to anyone himself?"

"No, I cannot. For one thing, Max is an avowed pacifist. I remember hearing that he was a conscientious objector during World War I. It is not something I have ever heard him talk about, but apparently he did his service in a military hospital or drove an ambulance, or maybe both. But he did not carry arms."

"Admirable," Wolfe said. "Mr. Breckenridge came to me because he said he had some vague feeling of unease about the production. Do you have any thoughts as to what may have been the cause of that unease?"

Peters shrugged. "I really felt things were going quite well. The rehearsals went smoothly, more so than in the other plays that I have been involved with. And the performances also seemed to go on without any serious snags. I have no idea what Mr. Breckenridge could have been concerned about."

"Steve, he must have feared someone or something," Lewis Hewitt said. "And those fears, whatever they may have been, certainly were justified as it turned out."

"I guess so," the young actor replied. "I'm afraid that I have not been much help to you. I simply can't explain any of it." Peters looked absolutely miserable.

"We appreciate your having come here tonight, however," Hewitt said, aware that Wolfe was unlikely to do much thanking. Saul escorted the young actor down the hall to the front door, and I left the alcove and went to the office, thankful once again to get off my feet.

"Some impressions?" I asked Wolfe after Saul had returned from his doorkeeper duties.

"The young man articulated it best. He was of little or no help. Your thoughts, Saul?"

"I agree. He seems younger than his years, and more than a little naive, which I find unusual in an actor. Either that or he is putting on one hell of an act as the wide-eyed male ingénue. And he also was nervous. I could smell the perspiration. He must have been sopping when he walked out of here."

"The guy acted pretty much the same when I talked to him," I said. "He was self-deprecating, referring to himself as 'a small cog' in the operation. He talked about all the razzing that he took from the old pros, who called him a 'Yalie' because he graduated from the drama school at Yale."

"Did he resent the razzing?" Saul asked.

"I got the impression he did at first, but he said he considered the kidding to be good-natured. He also admitted to being nervous early on in the production but said he gained confidence as he settled in."

"Why would he have been nervous?" Saul posed. "He had been in Broadway plays before."

"He claimed he was intimidated by the presence of Ashley Williston and Brad Lester in the cast. But he said part of the reason he became more confident was that Williston took him under her wing."

"She probably wanted to take more than that," Saul said. "And who knows, maybe she did."

"Could be," I said, turning to Wolfe. "That is something to ask the lady. She will be our guest tomorrow at eleven."

He grunted, got to his feet, and left the office, wishing us a good evening.

"Well, does anyone want to give odds on Mr. Peters's guilt?" I asked Saul and Hewitt.

"For some reason, don't ask me why, I don't trust him," Saul said. "It wasn't just his nervousness; a certain amount of that is understandable. I felt he was being . . . evasive."

"I think I agree with Saul," Hewitt said, "although part of that may well be the difficult position Ashley has put him in."

"Yeah, he undoubtedly does not want to talk about her attempts to seduce him," I added.

"And maybe, just maybe, they were more than *attempts*," Saul said.

"So Mr. Peters has his hands full dealing with Ashley Williston. What about him as a murderer?" I asked.

"I just don't see how the two things are connected," Hewitt said.

"Neither do I," I answered, "but something is definitely eating at Steve Peters."

# CHAPTER 24

The next morning, I settled in at my desk with coffee after having devoured a breakfast of Fritz's brioches and grilled ham, along with a blueberry muffin and orange juice. I was working on the orchid germination records when the phone rang.

"Nero Wolfe's office, Archie Goodwin speaking."

"Of course it is. Who else would be answering?" Lon Cohen said.

"What can I do for you, gazetteer of the goings-on of the great, the near great, and the not so great?"

"*Gazetteer*, is it? You have been around Nero Wolfe too long. He is the only person I know who would use such a word."

"Now you know two who would, and besides, where do you think the name of your very own and esteemed newspaper comes from? Now, to what do we owe the honor of this call?"

"I trust that you have not seen our early edition?"

"No, our *Gazette* gets delivered around noon. Until then, we are forced to subsist on a diet of the *Times*."

"The almighty and exalted *Times*, however, did not carry an item that we did, which is an item I believe you and your boss will find most interesting."

"Is this a guessing game?"

"No, guessing is what I have to do when trying to figure out why you and Wolfe are so interested in the late Roy Breckenridge."

"I believe Mr. Wolfe said you would be the first to know about any developments involving Mr. Breckenridge's death—that is, if we are even working on a case involving him."

"I am going to guess that you are, and I am also going to guess that an ad in today's edition will pique your and your boss's interests."

"Try me."

"On page twelve, main news section, lower right-hand corner, full-page width, five inches deep, bordered in black, is a box containing the following: '*Wanted: Information Pertaining to the Death of Producer Roy Breckenridge. Reward: $50,000, payable at the discretion of Ashley Williston. Direct all responses to: Box 21*, the New York Gazette.'"

"I will be damned."

"I am sure that you will. One of her stipulations in placing the ad was that no one on our editorial staff be allowed to interview her. Our hands are tied."

"Cheer up. That ad must have brought at least a few thousand shekels into the *Gazette*'s coffers."

"Cheer up, my foot. Did Wolfe bankroll it? He's been known to buy space in the papers before."

"No comment."

"Is he in touch with Williston?"

"No comment."

"Come on, Archie, give me something here. You know that every other paper in town is going to be after her, and we could very well end up getting scooped on our own bloody ad."

"I doubt that very much. Do you know whether any of the other papers are carrying the ad?"

"No, and neither does our advertising department. It was not in this morning's *Times* or *Daily News*, and we'll be scouring the other afternoon papers when they hit the street, of course."

"If I were to speculate, I would say the lady chose your paper and your paper only."

"But why not the *Daily News*? It's got more readers than we do. And so does the *Times*, although not by much."

"Maybe she figures your readers are the ones who would be more likely to know something about Breckenridge's death. After all, the *Gazette* has the fifth-largest circulation in the country, never mind that those two other rags you just mentioned are bigger. And you have the best Broadway coverage of any daily in town. I know that because you've told me so on several occasions."

"Thank you for that acknowledgment. By the way, you must not call the *Times* a 'rag,' Archie. Try to show at least a little respect for our worthy competitor."

"Sorry, I got carried away. Back to the subject at hand, I believe I speak for Mr. Wolfe in saying that if and when we have any information regarding the Breckenridge death, you will be the first publication to know."

"Where have I heard that line before?"

"I cannot imagine. Stay tuned."

No sooner had I hung up than the instrument rang again. It was Inspector Cramer.

"Did Wolfe place that damned ad in the *Gazette*?" he roared.

"No, he did not, that much I can assure you. When he does run newspaper advertising, he directs all responses to himself."

"Huh! Have you been in touch with the Williston dame?"

"Not recently," I told him, which would still be the truth for a couple more hours.

"Has Wolfe gotten anywhere at all on the Breckenridge business?"

"No sir, unless he knows things he has not chosen to share with me. Would you like him to call you?" My answer was a hang-up. I then dialed Wolfe in the plant rooms.

"Yes?" He hates to be disturbed when he's playing with the orchids, or the "concubines," as he calls them.

"Sorry to bother you, but since we are seeing Ashley Williston just after you descend from on high, you should know about this advertisement that is running in the *Gazette* today." I read it to him, word for word.

Wolfe cursed, a rarity for him. "I will be down at eleven," he said, hanging up. Everybody seemed to be slamming down their receiver on me. At this rate, I could get a complex.

Saul Panzer and Lewis Hewitt came to the brownstone at 10:45, and I told them about the Williston ad in the *Gazette*.

"Leave it to Ashley to stir things up," Hewitt said, shaking his head. "With the show at least temporarily shuttered, she is desperate for publicity."

"You mean this move isn't out of the goodness of her heart?" Saul asked with a wry grin.

"Hah! All of us know better," the Long Island orchid grower replied. "If you look up *opportunist* in the dictionary, you are likely to see her picture along with the definition."

"We already knew her meeting with Wolfe was going to be

interesting," I put in, "and with this latest development, it could be one of the better spectator sports events of the year."

"There's the doorbell," Saul said. "Looks like it's time for you to go into hiding again, Archie."

And so I did. Saul escorted Ashley into the office, and from my hiding place, I saw her sweep in with a flourish that any director or stage manager would give a thumbs-up.

The actress was clad in a royal-blue suit, blue pumps, and a ruffled white blouse. She looked like she had just stepped out of a magazine spread for Saks or Lord & Taylor.

"Hello, Lewis," she said to Hewitt, who stood. "Where is this famous Nero Wolfe I am supposed to see?"

"He will be here shortly."

"I am here now," Wolfe said, entering the office, settling into the chair behind his desk, and placing a raceme of orchids in a vase as Hewitt directed Ashley to the red leather chair. "Would you like something to drink, madam? Coffee or tea perhaps? I am having beer."

"Nothing, thank you," she said coolly, crossing one nylon-sheathed leg over the other. "I did not come here to socialize."

"I admire your candor and also your businesslike attitude," he told her. "You purchased an advertisement that is running in today's *Gazette*."

"I did. After all, someone had to do something. The police seem to have gotten nowhere, and if you have made any progress, I have yet to hear about it."

"I am proceeding with my investigation," Wolfe said, opening one of the two bottles of beer Fritz had just brought in and pouring some into a frosted glass.

"I certainly am glad to hear that, but just what do you have to show for your work? And has the mysterious Mr. MacGregor been located? It seems to me that he could be the solution to Roy's death."

"For reasons I cannot elaborate on at present, I can assure you Mr. MacGregor is not a factor in the death of Roy Breckenridge," Wolfe said.

"Will you give me your word on that?"

"I could, but I know what my word is worth, and you do not."

The actress frowned. "I restate my earlier question: Have you made any progress whatever?"

"Some, although I am not prepared to report at the moment. Now I will turn the tables and become the questioner. What do you expect to learn from the advertisement?"

"That should be obvious. I am hoping someone will come forward with information about Roy's murder."

"Obvious? I think not. When you use fifty thousand dollars as bait, you will get a mighty poor grade of fish as your catch. Those responding will concoct myriad scenarios in order to collect a reward."

"Ah, but you have failed to see a stipulation in the ad," she said in a triumphant tone. "'Payable at the discretion of Ashley Williston.'"

"I have made note of your stipulation, madam. Notwithstanding its inclusion, you are likely to become bombarded with preposterous dramaturgy. You also run the risk of incurring the wrath of the police department."

"What do I care about the police department?" Ashley snapped, dismissing the entire force with a stagy hand gesture. "It appears to me that they have done nothing. I am told Inspector Cramer is a good policeman, and also a smart one, but I have yet to see progress of any kind on the part of either the man or his foot soldiers. And as to incurring the department's wrath, I understand that, over the years, you have done a good deal of that yourself."

"I have, but not recklessly, as is the case with this advertisement. Mr. Cramer, whom I have known for years, is indeed a good man, and it would not be wise to poke him in the eye with a stick. Setting the advertisement aside for now, do you have any theories as to Mr. Breckenridge's assailant?"

"None. To my knowledge, Roy had no enemies. Other producers were envious of his success, of course, but professional envy is hardly a stimulus for murder. If that were the case, Broadway would be littered with the corpses of actors, directors, and producers."

"Well put," Wolfe said. "How would you describe your working relationship with Mr. Breckenridge?"

"Mine?" she said, wide-eyed, fluttering a slender, manicured hand to her breast. "We always got along, we understood each other. I had known Roy for years and had been in a couple of his other productions."

"Did you respect his expertise?"

"Of course I did, and just why wouldn't I?"

"I understand you frequently questioned his directorial decisions, sometimes in the presence of others, during rehearsals for *Death at Cresthaven*."

She leaned forward, lips pursed, and placed a hand on his desk. "Who told you that?" she demanded.

"Is it true?"

"Uh, I did make a few suggestions from time to time, nothing that I would call major changes."

"How did Mr. Breckenridge react to your suggestions?"

"He agreed with some, disagreed with others," she said. "I do not see where this is relevant."

"Perhaps it is not," Wolfe conceded. "Did you enjoy amicable relations with others in the cast?"

"Amicable? I suppose so. They all knew their lines and were well prepared, at least most of the time. That goes a long way toward ensuring good relations on any production."

"How did you feel about Mr. Lester, a newcomer to what is termed legitimate theater, joining the company?"

Ashley inhaled. "I will be honest. I did not know what to expect, given his lack of stage experience," she said. "In the time since Brad joined us, I must say I have been pleasantly surprised."

"Do you have thoughts as to why Mr. Breckenridge chose him?"

More inhaling. "All I can surmise is that Roy felt his name had . . . box-office appeal."

"There were others in the cast—albeit two of them young— who had Broadway credits, yourself, of course, included. Do you feel it was necessary for the producer to choose a man whose career was defined by motion pictures?"

"I do not know the answer, Mr. Wolfe," she said stiffly.

"Did you ever raise that question with Mr. Breckenridge?"

"I do recall being somewhat surprised at the choice, and in fact, I did ask Roy about it. He said, 'I always like to take chances, and I'm taking one on Brad. I think he's got what it takes to handle the role.'"

"Did it bother you that Mr. Lester was billed ahead of you?"

"I find that question to be offensive!"

"Why? I should think you would have had every right to be offended that you were not given top billing. Given your experience, it would have been a natural reaction from one who has a healthy sense of self."

"I don't have to take this from you any longer," she said, standing.

"Sit down, Ashley!" Lewis Hewitt said, now on his feet. "This is a murder investigation. You cannot just walk out of here!"

"Investigation—by a private eye? What kind of an investigation is that?" she fired back, small fists clenched.

"I said, sit down!" I had known Hewitt for a number of

years, albeit not well, and I had always considered him to be genial and gregarious, but this was a side of the man I had not seen. I could tell even Wolfe was impressed by his commanding demeanor and was thankful for it.

Ashley Williston sat, teeth clenched and hands in her lap, looking like a petulant child. She clearly knew Hewitt was now the key to her future, at least as far as *Death at Cresthaven* was concerned.

"Assuming you get information you feel is germane from the advertisement, do you plan to share it with the police?" Wolfe asked.

She smiled tightly. "I suppose so, of course. Were you hoping I would share it with you?"

"Only if you saw fit."

"I have been doing some research on you, Mr. Wolfe," Ashley said, "and I have learned that you have a longtime assistant named Archie Goodwin. Yet he is not here. Not that there is anything wrong with your man Mr. Panzer, whom I have just met," she said, favoring Saul with a thin smile.

"Mr. Goodwin is otherwise occupied."

"Of course. I am sure you often handle several cases at once. Do you have anything else to ask me?"

"Not at present."

"Well, I have something to ask you—all of you, really. What is the current condition of poor Max?"

"He remains comatose, and his condition continues to be critical, but stable," Hewitt said.

"Well, that is something, anyway. May I leave now, Lewis?" she asked. "Or do any of you have further questions?"

Hewitt looked at Wolfe, who moved his head back and forth a fraction of an inch. "I do not. Thank you for coming. Mr. Panzer will show you out."

Ashley rose smoothly and glided from the room without a backward look, as if she were leaving the stage at the close of an act. The only thing missing was applause.

I got back to the office and had settled in at my desk when Saul returned from escorting Ashley Williston to the front door. "You certainly took your time," I said. "Did the lady beguile you?"

"You know how it is, Archie. Some got it, some don't. I just happen to be one of the lucky ones."

"Yeah, put me down as envious."

"If we can dispense with the raillery, I would like each of your thoughts regarding Miss Williston," Wolfe said as he polished off his second beer.

"You mean you are actually soliciting our opinions?" I asked, feigning surprise. "Okay, I will go first: When I met her during my time masquerading as Alan MacGregor, boy reporter, I thought she was arrogant, self-centered, and narcissistic. Watching her today only confirmed my original appraisal. As to whether she is capable of murder, my vote is still out."

"But if she *were* the murderer," Hewitt said, "would she spend a substantial amount on an advertisement soliciting information about the killing?"

"That might be just the thing a murderer would do to deflect suspicion from oneself," Panzer put in. "Besides, she figures to be a wealthy woman. The ad's cost would hardly put a dent in her pocketbook."

"I must agree with Saul," Wolfe said. "A wily murderer— and our Miss Williston manifestly possesses wiles—might well behave as she has. This woman is a machinator."

"Interesting that she took notice of Archie's absence," Hewitt observed. "Do you feel she added things up and came to the conclusion that he and Alan MacGregor are one and the same?"

"I do not," Wolfe said. "She is far too self-absorbed to make such a deduction."

"You have the rest of the day to recover from Miss Williston's visit before the arrival of yet another female in the brownstone," I told Wolfe. "Melissa Cartwright will come calling at nine tonight."

He answered with a glower.

# CHAPTER 25

I found myself increasingly space deprived, given that I had spent so much time on my feet in that alcove no larger than a Manhattan telephone booth—make that a *small* Manhattan phone booth. The good news was that I probably would have to use the peephole only two or three more times during this case: to observe the interviews with Melissa Cartwright tonight and Brad Lester tomorrow morning and—just maybe—to watch over a gathering of the whole crew in the office for what Cramer refers to as one of Wolfe's "charades."

"Tell me your thoughts about this young Cartwright woman," Saul Panzer asked me as we sat in the office with Lewis Hewitt a few minutes before she was scheduled to arrive.

"She is young, close to thirty, attractive although not what I would term beautiful, and enthusiastic about her burgeoning career. She has a freshness about her that borders on naïveté,

which means she can easily play an ingénue. Would you agree?"
I asked Hewitt.

"Pretty much. I can't say that I know her well at all, but she
seems to make friends quickly and be easy to work with. She—"

The doorbell rang, my cue to disappear yet again. From the
peephole, I watched Saul escort Melissa into the office and get her
seated in the red leather chair. She wore low-heeled white sandals
and a simple and demure light-green summer dress that went well
with her red hair. She nodded and said a soft hello to Hewitt and
then looked around the office in awe, focusing on the big Gouchard
world globe with its diameter of thirty-two-plus inches. Here we
had the ideal suspect in a classic whodunit mystery, the person
least likely to commit a murder, I thought. She is a picture of fresh-
faced innocence—in other words, the perfect killer.

Wolfe walked into the office, dipped his chin slightly in our
guest's direction, and got himself seated while placing yellow
*Odontoglossums* in the vase on his desk. He asked our guest if
she desired something to drink—she didn't—then pushed the
buzzer for beer, which Fritz delivered. If Melissa was surprised
at Wolfe's appearance, she did not show it.

"I trust it has not been an inconvenience for you to come
here today," he said.

"No sir, not in the least; I will do anything I can to help. All
of this has been awful," she replied, licking her lips.

"You are among the younger players in the *Death at
Cresthaven* cast. Have the more senior members of the troupe
treated you well?"

"Oh, they have, by all means," she said, nodding vigorously.

"How would you describe your relations with Mr.
Breckenridge?" Wolfe asked.

Melissa took a deep breath before answering. "He was a very
encouraging person, very positive."

"Did everyone else involved with the production get along well with him?"

"As far as I know," she said, nodding again.

"How about Miss Williston? She is in possession of a very strong personality."

"Ashley has . . . a lot of ideas, and she wants to share them."

"Good ideas?"

"Some of them are. But on occasion, Mr. Breckenridge reminded her—nicely, of course—that he was the director."

"How did she react to these squelches?"

"Well, I would not call them *squelches* exactly," Melissa said, shifting in her chair. "They were really more like gentle reminders that he was the one in charge. These reminders caused Ashley to become, well . . . I would say more subdued."

"And not altogether happy?"

"Yes, that's true." She looked at Hewitt and then at Saul as if seeking affirmation. "Um . . . might I have some water?"

Wolfe dipped his chin at Saul, who went to the kitchen, coming back in less than a minute with a glass of water with ice.

"Thank you," she said. "I'm battling a summer cold. You know how it is, going from the heat outside to air-conditioning and then back to the heat again, et cetera."

Wolfe did not know, of course, as he rarely left home. He waited a few seconds before continuing. "Overall, would you say the morale of the cast was high?"

Yet another nod. "It seemed like it to me. I've been in a few Broadway productions before, and I would say this was pretty typical of the morale in those other shows."

"Can you conceive of any reason someone would want to kill Mr. Breckenridge?"

"No, I cannot, sir," she said, kneading her small hands in her lap.

"Who were you closest to in the cast?"

Melissa closed her eyes, as if thinking about the question. "I guess . . . it would have to be Max—Mr. Ennis."

"Indeed? Why was that?"

"Well, I confided in him when I had a problem. He was a good listener and very sympathetic."

"What was the nature of these confidences?"

"Mostly involving my family back in Michigan. After thirty-five years of marriage, my parents are getting a divorce, and I am sick about it, but I could not return home because of our performance schedule."

"What about now? The show is in abeyance."

She sighed. "The only good thing about what has happened is that I am able to return to Lansing. I'm taking the train there in a few days, and I will try to get them to reconcile, but I am not optimistic."

"Back to Mr. Ennis. Can you think of a reason why he would attempt to kill himself?"

"No, I can't, unless it was because of his health. Max seemed to be in pain much of the time, although he did an awfully good job of hiding it, especially when he was onstage."

"Did he discuss his condition with you?"

"No, never. He was always willing to listen to my problems, but he never shared his own troubles with me. He was a very self-sufficient individual. I asked him once if there was anything I could do, but he seemed embarrassed by the question and the attention, and he insisted he was fine, although I knew that definitely was not the case."

"Do you find it unusual that arsenic, probably in rat poison, was involved both in Mr. Breckenridge's death and Mr. Ennis's apparent suicide attempt?"

"I was not aware of that."

"One might be tempted to make the case that Max Ennis poisoned Mr. Breckenridge and then utilized the same substance in an attempt to do away with himself."

"I don't believe it!" Melissa said, leaning forward and showing emotion for the first time.

"Did you not tell the police you overheard Messrs. Breckenridge and Ennis having a heated argument?" Wolfe asked.

"Yes, yes, I did. I heard them in Max's dressing room as I was walking down the hall. I couldn't make out what they were saying, and I didn't want to eavesdrop, but they both sounded angry, very angry."

"Did you mention this to anyone?"

"Uh . . . yes, I did. I told that policeman, the one who always seems to be angry himself."

"Inspector Cramer?"

"Yes, that's the man."

"In his job, he has a lot to be angry about," Saul said.

"After hearing this exchange, did you observe anything backstage or perhaps in rehearsals that suggested a reason for the apparent animosity?" Wolfe posed.

"No, nothing that I could see, sir."

"How would you describe your relationship to Mr. Peters?"

Melissa looked surprised. "Steve? Why do you ask?"

"He is the person nearest your age in the cast. I am curious as to whether that may have drawn you closer together."

"Well, we are close to the same age, of course, and Steve is a very likable person. So I guess you could say we've become somewhat friendly as we've gotten to know each other."

"How would you define 'somewhat friendly'?"

That brought color to her cheeks. "I am not sure what you mean."

"Come now, Miss Cartwright. Did your friendship extend beyond what might be expected in an amiable professional relationship?"

"I do not really think that is anyone's business," she said with a sniff. Her primness was getting on my nerves.

"Normally, I would agree," Wolfe replied evenly. "However, this is a discussion involving a murder along with what appears to be a suicide attempt. I am sure the police already have asked you questions that made you uncomfortable."

"They did not ask me about Steve."

"But I am."

"I think I would like to leave now," she said, easing out of her chair.

"Melissa, please sit down and answer Mr. Wolfe," Hewitt told her in a tone that was at once both soft and firm.

She sat. "I am finding this very uncomfortable," the actress said. *Whatever else you do, don't start crying*, I thought. If she did, Wolfe would then march out of the room.

"Go on," Hewitt urged her.

"Steve and I . . . We like each other, quite a lot."

"Was this mutual attraction obvious to others in the company?" Wolfe asked.

"I really don't think so. By design, we rarely spoke to each other backstage or downstairs, except when necessary. At those times we spent together, meeting for a lunch or taking a walk, it was always far from the theater, often down in the Village, where others from the cast were not likely to go."

"It has been suggested that Miss Williston was attracted to Mr. Peters."

"Who told you that?"

"The source is irrelevant," Wolfe said. "Is it true?"

"She is not a terribly nice person," Melissa replied, taking a deep breath. "Have you spoken to her?"

"I have."

"Then you must know what she is like," Melissa said, anger now creeping into her voice.

"How did Mr. Peters react to the woman's advances?"

"He hated it, he absolutely hated it! He told me Ashley made his flesh crawl—that is exactly the phrase he used. But he felt he had to maintain good relations with her. After all, she does have a lot of influence in the theater community, and it is not smart to get on her bad side."

"Did he tell you what 'maintaining good relations with her' entailed?"

"Not in so many words, but I have now come to know Steve well enough to be absolutely positive that he had no interest whatever in the so-called charms of Miss Ashley Williston."

"It would seem the intrigues among members of the production have led to a high degree of tension."

Melissa pursed her lips and nodded. "It is natural to come to that conclusion, all right. However, rehearsals always went fairly smoothly, and the relatively few performances we staged before . . . before what happened were well received, both by reviewers and the audiences. It seemed like we were going to have a long run, until, well . . ."

"If this production is forced to close down permanently, what will you do?" Wolfe asked.

"I suppose I will try to find something else on Broadway, if I am lucky. Otherwise, perhaps a production in some smaller theater, hopefully right here in New York. I can tell you this: I certainly do not want to go back home to Lansing permanently, under any circumstances."

"I must excuse myself and tend to other business," Wolfe said, rising and walking out without another word.

Melissa looked at Hewitt and then at Panzer with a puzzled expression. "Did I offend him?"

"It was not anything you said," Saul assured her. "Mr. Wolfe tends toward brevity and does not indulge in small talk."

"Mr. Panzer is right," Hewitt added. "Thank you so much for coming."

"Do you think there is any hope that the show will start up again?" she asked him.

"That is very hard to say right now, but I would not count on it. I wish I could be more optimistic."

Melissa got to her feet, wearing a glum expression as Saul escorted her out.

# CHAPTER 26

By the time I had emerged from my hiding place and stepped into the office, Saul and Hewitt were evaluating Melissa Cartwright's performance. "She is just too cute by half," Saul was saying. "That Miss Prissy act of hers wears pretty darn thin pretty darn quickly."

"However, I do believe she is genuine," Hewitt countered. "True, I don't know the young woman all that well, but it seems to me she's really rattled by all that has happened in this star-crossed show."

"What about you, Archie?" Saul said. "You are an expert on attractive young women. I know that to be true because you have told me so on many more occasions than I can count."

"Aw, shucks," I replied. "I am just a country boy from the rolling hills of southern Ohio."

"Speaking of acts that are wearing pretty thin. Out with it: Give us your reading on Miss Cartwright?"

"I would be more interested in hearing Wolfe's reading on her, but he has fled the scene and is likely hunkered down in the kitchen bedeviling Fritz, so that will have to wait. However, since you asked, I think there is more to the young lady than meets the eye. She is attractive, no question. And those dimples of hers did not escape my notice the first time we met, back in the days when I was known as Alan MacGregor, Canadian magazine writer. But I can't help but feel she is holding something back."

"Well, she did own up to her interest in young Mr. Peters," Hewitt said, "although Wolfe had to pry it out of her."

"True, but that intimacy alone is hardly a crime in itself," Saul remarked. "After all, the two play a couple in the production, so it is hardly surprising that their intimate stage relationship might have carried over into the larger world. It has happened countless times before, both on Broadway and in Hollywood. Marriages have resulted from such pairings."

"Speaking of Hollywood, Wolfe still has one more person to interview," I said. "Brad Lester, he of what the magazines call the silver screen."

"You both have met him," Saul said to us. "What is your take?"

"Overall, I have been impressed," Hewitt said. "I haven't talked all that much to Lester, but I have seen him twice in the production and watched a few of the rehearsals. He is a first-rate professional and seems easy to get along with. He doesn't appear to have a lot of baggage—and by that I mean an inflated ego."

"I agree with Mr. Hewitt," I said. "When I interviewed him, I found him to be gregarious and unimpressed with himself. I am sure the man has got an ego, but overall, he seems to do a good job of suppressing it."

"What about his relationship with Ashley Williston?" Saul posed.

"Ah, now there is the question. When Wolfe and I talked to

Breckenridge in what now seems like ages ago, he told us Ashley was so nasty to Lester that, at one point, the actor was heard to say 'I'd like to strangle that bitch.'"

"She certainly seems to have the capacity to bring out the worst in people," Saul observed.

"Yeah," I agreed, "and when I asked Lester about her, he was a little slow in responding. Being a good performer, he recovered quickly and praised her professionalism. And he was unstinting in his praise for Breckenridge, crediting him with taking a gamble on a film star. If he had a reason for killing the producer, I'm darned if I can see it. And then—"

I was interrupted by the phone. I answered and was greeted with the belligerent tones of Inspector Cramer. "I assume you want to speak to Mr. Wolfe," I said.

"No, you will do. Since I still think Wolfe had a hand in that ad the Williston dame stuck in the *Gazette*, I thought both of you would like know about the kind of garbage it drew, and you can pass this along to your boss."

"We've told you that Mr. Wolfe did not have anything to do with—"

"I know, so you say. Here's one response, from a woman who signs herself as Mrs. Williams of Larchmont. 'I attended a matinee of *Death at Cresthaven*, and it is obvious to me, as it should be to any other theatergoer, who killed Mr. Breckenridge. It was that awful Reed woman, of course, who played the maid, Olive. She was given terrible lines to speak, and people I overheard in the audience were laughing at her, making fun of her. There's your murderer.'"

"Very interesting, but—"

"You need to hear these," Cramer cut in. "Here's one from a C. Logan of Staten Island. He says, 'A lady friend of mine happens to be a neighbor of Ashley Williston on the Upper East

Side, and a few weeks ago, we attended a cocktail party that the Williston woman attended. She'd had a few cocktails and began to make comments, and very snide comments they were, about Roy Breckenridge and how he was undermining her by putting a Hollywood star in the cast and giving him the top billing. She got so angry that the hostess asked her, politely of course, to leave, which she did, but not quietly. If you are looking for a killer, you've got her.'

"One last response, Goodwin," Cramer said before I could get in a word. "This one is from Alan Blake of Brooklyn, who says 'I was not surprised about what happened to Roy Breckenridge. I happen to know one of the stagehands who works on the show, and he said there had been bad blood between Breckenridge and this movie star Brad Lester almost from the start. He claims he heard an angry Lester tell Breckenridge after a performance that "Your problem here is with your cast. You told me I would be well accepted, and that has not been the case. You have sold me a false bill of goods." So it's obvious that this Lester is the killer.'"

"Inspector, I —"

"I am not done, Goodwin. So far, Ashley Williston has brought us twenty-two responses to her ad. Here are the votes as murderer: Lester, five; Williston, three; Peters, three; Cartwright, three; Reed, three; Sperry, two; Ennis, two; and a stagehand named Quigley, one. Now isn't that just dandy?"

"One question, Inspector: How does Miss Williston feel about these responses, given that she herself is tied for second place in the balloting?"

"The woman is hardly happy," Cramer said, "and I think she's beginning to regret that she took out that damned ad. I asked her if she was giving us all the responses, and she swore she was. I'll repeat what I said before: This whole business was a stupid idea."

"I agree. And I also will repeat what I said before: Nero Wolfe had nothing to do with buying that space in the *Gazette*."

Cramer said something I will not repeat and hung up on me. I turned to the others and gave them a summary of our conversation.

Saul laughed. "It would have been even funnier if Ashley had gotten the most votes," he said. "Still, tied for second isn't all that bad."

Hewitt shook his head. "What a mess. That silliness with the advertisement didn't accomplish a thing. Quite the contrary."

"Yeah, and Cramer still seems convinced Mr. Wolfe placed the ad," I said. "So much for tonight. We'll reconvene tomorrow for the visit from Brad Lester."

"I can hardly wait," Lewis Hewitt said, although his tone lacked conviction.

# CHAPTER 27

I was in the office the next morning at 10:45, finishing the typing of a batch of correspondence for Wolfe, when the doorbell sounded. It was Saul and Mr. Hewitt. "Well, gentlemen," I said when we were seated in the office with coffee, "this is it, our final interview. Are both of you prepared to spend time with a real-life honest-to-goodness movie star?"

"I will try to control my excitement," Saul told me. "Although, according to what you have told us, the guy seems to be a regular joe."

"Yes, as I said before, that was my impression. I am sure one of you will correct me if you find I have erred in my judgment of the man."

"You both will recall that I also am on record as having been impressed with Mr. Lester," Hewitt said. "We will rely upon Mr. Panzer and Mr. Wolfe for fresh perspectives on the actor."

The bell sounded again, and once more, I disappeared from the office while Saul sauntered down the hall to the front door. From my all-too-familiar cranny, I watched as Brad Lester ambled into the office wearing a smile. "Mr. Hewitt, it's good to see you," he boomed, shaking hands with the man who might soon become his boss, assuming *Death at Cresthaven* would eventually be restaged.

Lester looked like a million bucks, but that was hardly surprising, given that his appearance was a major part of his persona: perfectly barbered black hair, likely dyed; a camel-hair sport coat and dark brown slacks; a dark brown, open-collared shirt; a paisley silk ascot; and those cowboy boots he had worn when I interviewed him.

The actor settled into the red leather chair like he owned it just as Nero Wolfe entered the office. "Good morning, sir," Wolfe said to the guest as he settled in behind his desk. The usual offer of a beverage was proffered and Lester politely declined. "Before we get started, how is Max Ennis?" Lester asked, leaning forward with his hands on his knees.

"Stable but still comatose," Hewitt replied. "His stomach was pumped, of course, but he had the poison in him for some time before the medics got to him. If he does eventually recover, no telling what he will be like."

"The poor guy," Lester said with what sounded to be genuine concern.

"You are fond of Mr. Ennis," Wolfe said.

"I am, although I can't really say I knew him all that well. He had not been in good health, as all of us knew. But he seemed to overcome any pain he was dealing with once he got onstage. It was inspiring to see."

"Do you believe he poisoned Mr. Breckenridge and then attempted suicide?"

"The suicide part I can believe, but Max a killer, never!" Lester said with feeling.

"Why do you think he would attempt suicide?"

He shook his head. "I can only suppose that it was because of his deteriorating health."

"Do you know if Messrs. Breckenridge and Ennis quarreled at any time during the rehearsals and the performances?"

"If they did, I never was aware of it. They seemed to get along well, and I believe they had known each other for some years. For that matter, Max probably knew almost everybody in the Broadway community, which is not surprising. He'd been around for decades."

"Do you have any nominees for the murderer?"

Lester chewed on his lip. "I really don't know whether Roy had enemies, but then, I am a newcomer to this world, Mr. Wolfe. I'm still learning my way around."

"It has been reported that you had some harsh words for Mr. Breckenridge about others in the cast."

"Really?" the actor said, stiffening. "Who said that?"

Wolfe ignored the question. "Is it true?"

Lester paused for several seconds, then let out air with a sigh. "I do recall saying something to Roy about . . . well, about one of the cast members."

"Miss Williston?"

"I guess it is hardly a secret that Ashley was resentful of my presence in the cast, particularly early on."

"For what reason?"

"*Reasons*, really. She seemed to have an aversion to Hollywood and anyone who makes a living in the movie business. Also, I quickly learned about her anger over the fact that I was billed ahead of her."

"Do you feel that anger was justified?" Saul asked.

"Possibly. After all, she had a long and generally successful career onstage, while, as I said, I am the new guy on the block, so to speak."

"Why do you feel you received the top billing?" Wolfe asked.

"There was an article about *Death at Cresthaven* in *Variety* just a few days before we opened. It quoted an unnamed 'Broadway observer' as saying that the producer and backers of the show felt that I got brought in and billed at the top because I had box-office appeal."

"Do you believe that?"

"Yes, I do, at the risk of seeming immodest."

"Is it also true that, after either a rehearsal or a performance, you were overheard to say 'I'd like to strangle that bitch'?"

"You seem to have very good sources, Mr. Wolfe," Lester said ruefully.

"You do not deny saying that?"

"No, it's true, and I said that after Ashley had sabotaged one of my lines by cutting me off midsentence. And she did it in such a way that it looked like it was part of the script. I have worked very hard to get along with her, but she can be a trial, worse than any of the prima donnas I've been paired with in films, and that is saying something. Have you met Ashley?"

"I have," Wolfe said. "She is a singular individual."

That brought a laugh from the actor, who slapped his thigh. "Well said! That is certainly one way of putting it." He seemed far more relaxed than any of the others who had preceded him to the brownstone.

"So, Mr. Lester, you have no idea whatever as to who might have wished Mr. Breckenridge ill?"

"No, sir, I am afraid I do not have a clue. But we haven't talked yet about that magazine writer, MacGregor is his name, who was hanging around the set interviewing all of us for some Canadian magazine that turns out to have been a fabrication, according to the newspapers. Whatever his motives, he could be your man. Has he been located and questioned?"

"For reasons I am unable to go into at this time," Wolfe said, "it has become clear to me, and to the police as well, that Mr. MacGregor has no involvement whatever in the death of Roy Breckenridge. I believe Mr. Hewitt will agree."

Hewitt nodded, and Brad Lester wore a puzzled look. "Well, then, I guess I have no choice but to take your word for that," he said. "Is there anything else that you need from me?"

"Not at present," Wolfe said, rising and walking out of the office.

Lester appeared perplexed at his host's abrupt departure but did not comment. "As I asked Mr. Wolfe before he left, is there anything else you need from me?"

"Not right now, Brad," Hewitt said. "Thank you for coming."

"Do you think there's any chance at all that Max will recover and that *Cresthaven* will reopen?" the actor asked.

"I wish I could answer one or both of those questions, but I cannot," Hewitt told him. "If you want to return to California for the time being, I see no need for you to stay here until everything gets sorted out, which may take some time."

"No, I believe I will hang around until something gets decided one way or another. I find I'm enjoying New York more every day, and this situation, sad as it may be, is a good opportunity for me to see lots of plays. I am getting to like the idea of the theater, and there's a lot of it to see here. Besides, I can throw on a pair of sunglasses and walk all over town without being recognized. I can't do that in L.A., not that people out there do much walking anyway. They drive everywhere, even if their destination is only a block from home. I'm getting more exercise than I have in years."

"So at least something good has come of all this," Hewitt said. "Enjoy this beautiful day, the best New York has to offer in the summer." Saul escorted Lester down the hall, and I made what I hope was my next-to-last exit from the alcove.

"What did you both think of Mr. Lester's performance?" I asked Saul and Hewitt when we reconvened in the office.

"Smooth, very smooth," Saul said. "Although I should not be surprised. I have seen him in a couple of films over the years, and he is solid, very self-possessed. Do I think he is capable of murder? I do. But what about in this particular situation? What could he possibly gain by poisoning Breckenridge? The producer had brought him east to help sell tickets with his screen reputation, and at a time when the onetime film idol's career was on the wane, by his own admission."

"I agree with Saul that Brad Lester did not appear to have a reason for killing Roy," Hewitt said. "If he were a violent man, which I seriously doubt, he would likely have directed his vitriol at Ashley Williston. No, I do not see Brad as the murderer."

"So where does that leave things," I asked, throwing my hands up, "other than my not having to stand in that alcove many more times?"

"It leaves things where it always does," Saul said, "in Mr. Wolfe's capable hands. You know as well as I do that he'll figure the whole business out—and sooner rather than later."

# CHAPTER 28

I was inclined to go along with Saul, but I failed to factor in one element: the dreaded relapse. Wolfe gets seized by one of these every few years, but like a hurricane, there is no way in hell of predicting when one will hit.

It was at eleven the next morning when I realized we were in relapse mode. Wolfe came down from the plant rooms as usual—so far, so good— but he showed no interest in the morning mail, and instead of ringing for beer, he marched out of the room after placing an orange orchid in the vase on his desk.

I waited ten minutes before sauntering into the kitchen. Wolfe was standing over Fritz, who was preparing a mushroom and almond omelet for lunch. "You want to add apricot jam?" Wolfe roared. "Unthinkable!"

Fritz started to argue, but he saw it was futile. He looked miserable, as is the case when Wolfe decides to play at being a chef, something he does often, particularly during relapses. On one of those occasions, I had to talk Fritz out of quitting, which would, of course, have been a calamity.

A few words about past relapses: They can last anywhere from a day to almost a week. I have never figured out what causes these, although they have occurred most often when Wolfe either loses interest in a case or has been stymied by one.

In some relapses, Wolfe eats prodigiously, even when measured by his own standards, such as the time he consumed half a sheep, cooked twenty different ways, in two days. And on another occasion, he quit drinking beer for three days.

It was too early to tell how long this relapse would drag on, but I had to find a way to put a stop to it, which would be like trying to stop a runaway semi without brakes going downhill.

These relapses are always hardest on Fritz, who, although Swiss, is possessed of a Gallic temperament—many of his forbears were French—and is easily upset. I already knew, based on past performances, that Wolfe would be eating today's lunch, and possible future meals, at the small table in the kitchen that is normally my breakfast spot. Where I would take morning nourishment became my problem, while Wolfe's constant presence in the kitchen was Fritz's problem. I went back to the office in disgust just as the phone was ringing, the house line, no less.

"Archie, it is Theodore. Can you come up to the plant rooms right now?"

In all the years I have lived and worked in the brownstone, I have never warmed to Theodore Horstmann, Wolfe's plant nurse, but that makes it even, because he has never liked me, either. On those rare occasions when I have been forced to go up to the plant rooms and interrupt Wolfe during one of his sessions with the orchids, Theodore has glared at me as if I were an unwelcome invader of the inner sanctum. Now he was inviting me to make the ascent, and in a civil tone, no less.

I walked up the three flights and entered orchid heaven, first the cool room, with its rows of yellow, red, and white-with-spots *Ondontoglossomus*; then the moderate room filled with *Cattleyas* of every color; and finally, the tropical room—*Miltonia* hybrids and *Philaenopsis* in pinks, browns, and greens. As often as I have passed through these halls, I never get used to the splendor. The rooms hold ten thousand orchids, or so Wolfe tells me. I have never counted them, so I will have to take his word, as I do on so many things.

Finally, I arrived in the potting room, where Theodore, clad in his apron and even more grim-faced than usual, stood, hands on hips, at one of the workbenches.

"Okay, so here I am," I told him. "What's the story?"

"I asked you to come up because I knew Mr. Wolfe would be downstairs, so we are free to talk," he said, shaking his head. "This is bad, very bad."

"How so?"

"It's the spell—he is having one of his spells," Theodore said in a shaky voice.

"He has had them before, as we both know all too well."

"Yes, but this one seems to be worse, Archie. After we were finished this morning, he said to me, 'I do not know when I will be back up here with you, Theodore. Take care of everything, you know very well where the problems are.' He has never said that to me before."

"I am every bit as frustrated as you are. Just what do you expect me to do?"

"Talk to him. Tell him the orchids need him."

"But you are very good with them yourself, aren't you? I know Mr. Wolfe places a great deal of trust in you. The flowers are not going to die because he doesn't come up here twice a day."

My words failed to mollify Theodore, who continued to wear a hangdog expression like one who has lost his best friend. "I just don't know what to do," he said, shaking his head and rubbing his hands together nervously. "I just don't know."

"Look, you are well aware that these moods of Mr. Wolfe's always pass. I am not sure how I can get him through this one quickly, but I will give it a shot." As I went back downstairs, I tried to figure out just what that shot would be.

Wolfe was still in the kitchen, sitting at the small table and sampling the omelet. "Fritz, I believe you are right after all," he said with the slightest trace of an apology in his voice. "Apricot jam is indeed called for. Let us make a new omelet."

"Will we be eating on time?" I asked to be sociable. My answer was a stony look from Wolfe, while Fritz looked more woebegone than ever.

"Okay, I got my answer. I'll grab some lunch over on Ninth Avenue."


"Hey, Archie, I haven't seen you for a while," said Herman, the owner and also the counterman at his fast-food joint, named Herman's, of course. "Looking for a culinary change of pace, eh?"

"I'm looking for one of your unequaled corned beef on rye sandwiches along with a glass of milk."

"In other words, the usual. What's going on in your world?"

"Murder, mayhem, double-dealing, and so on."

"In other words, also the usual. Well, the latest here is that I lost my longtime cook a week ago."

"Lenny? What happened—did he get a better offer?"

"He seemed to think so. He decided to open his own place up in Mount Vernon, an Italian joint, including pizza."

"But Lenny's Jewish."

"He is not about to let that stop him. What's really troubling, though, is that he just is not a good businessman. I will give him a year, eighteen months at the most, before he gives it up and goes bankrupt."

"Think he'll end up coming back here, trying to get his old job?"

Herman shook his head. "I doubt it, too much pride. Besides, I like the guy I've got working in the kitchen now, name's Ernest. He's good, he's fast, and he doesn't complain like Lenny did."

"So it seems to have turned out to your advantage. After I finish this wonderful sandwich, I have to go home and face a boss who is on strike, an unhappy chef, and an orchid gardener who is in a funk."

"Sure you don't want to hang around a little longer?" Herman said. "Can I tempt you with a slice of apple pie à la mode?"

"Sold—bring it on!"

# CHAPTER 29

I was in no hurry to get back to the brownstone, but I knew I could not put off my return indefinitely. I walked over to the Hudson and watched one of the Circle Line cruise boats loaded with tourists about to take off for its narrated trip around Manhattan, and part of me wished I were on board with them, taking in the wonders of our city from its rivers on a splendid afternoon. But I had work to do back on Thirty-Fifth Street, so I turned and headed home.

When I got back, I went straight to the office, where Wolfe sat at his desk perusing an orchid catalog that had come with the morning mail.

"Interesting reading you got there?" I asked as I sat at my own desk. No answer.

"Do I have any instructions?" Still no answer.

"Well, this certainly is an intriguing situation. Here we have a detective who claims to be a genius and who supposedly is working on a high-profile case, yet he does not seem to be working at all. Or am I missing something? Is that great brain, at this very moment, percolating and about to solve the murder of one of America's most renowned theatrical producers?"

Not a word from Wolfe. Just then the phone rang. "At last, maybe some excitement," I said to the only other person in the room, who remained engrossed in looking at pictures of orchids.

The caller was Lon Cohen. "Come on, Archie, give us something on the Breckenridge case, for God's sake, anything at all, if only to help out your friend Cramer. Every paper in town, including our own, is calling for his scalp, along with all of those civic groups that rail against crime, corruption, and the usual governmental ineptness."

"I've told you before that we are not in business to bail out Cramer when he is under fire. And if I had anything I could feed you, I would, but Nero Wolfe currently is in hibernation. Sorry, but there you have it."

"So I am supposed to order up a story that has the word 'hibernation' in it, and in the middle of summer, no less."

"Sorry, but as Walter Cronkite likes to sign off on his nightly news show, 'and that's the way it is.'"

The response I got from Lon is not worth sharing with you—and is one of those words not permitted on Cronkite's network news show.

"Lon sends his very best regards," I said to the sphinx who sat at his desk reading. Finally, I got what I thought was a bright idea. "I have two words for you," I told Wolfe. "They are *Grammangis spectabilis*." With that, he actually stirred, then set the catalog down and rose, walking out of the office to the elevator.

I waited ninety seconds, then called the plant rooms. When Theodore answered, I asked, "Is Mr. Wolfe up there with you?"

"No, Archie," he said in a dismal tone. "He is not here."

So he had gone to his room, presumably to get away from me, and also to avoid both Fritz and Theodore. This was indeed serious. He skipped lunch, although he had sampled the omelet, so he had taken at least some nourishment. The tests would be, first, whether he showed up in the plant rooms at four, and second, whether he came down for dinner.

Wolfe did not make it to the plant rooms, further upsetting Theodore, but he did ride the elevator down and walk into the office at 6:15, settling in behind his desk. He did not, however, ring for beer, so we still were in crisis mode. I pivoted and turned to him, prepared to make a smart remark, when I was stopped cold.

He had leaned back in the chair, hands interlaced over his stomach. His eyes were closed and his lips pushed out and in, out and in. He was somewhere else, in a place he probably couldn't describe himself. I took a deep breath and looked at my watch. For some reason, years ago, I had begun timing these episodes, and some of them went on for close to an hour. I did not care how long this one continued, I only knew the relapse had ended, and we were about to get back to business.

For the record, Wolfe's trance lasted a few seconds over forty-seven minutes. He jerked upright, blinked, and looked at me as if he were seeing me for the first time.

"Confound it, Archie, I have been a lackwit," he said with a snort. "The truth was right in front of me, and I steadfastly ignored it. I stand before you chagrined."

"Except that you are sitting," I said. That crack earned me a scowl, as well it should have.

"Call Lewis Hewitt. Call Saul. See if they both can come

tonight at nine," he said. "Use any means at your disposal to get them here."

As it turned out, I did not have to put my skills of persuasion to a test. Hewitt had planned to spend a quiet evening at home with his wife, and if Saul had anything planned, he didn't say so.

Dinner was veal birds in casserole, and after we had polished off two large helpings each, Wolfe lavished praise upon Fritz, who actually executed a slight bow. Apparently, any hard feelings over the day's earlier gastronomic controversy had dissipated, and order was restored in the brownstone.

Saul and Hewitt arrived promptly, no surprise. "These meetings are getting to be a habit, and I shall miss them," Hewitt said with a grin. "It is always stimulating to be around your boss."

"I can think of a few other adjectives to describe him," I replied.

"Aw, Archie, you love this life, and you know it," Saul said as we settled in the office awaiting Wolfe's arrival. He came in, dipped his chin slightly in greeting, and sat, ringing for beer.

"Saul, take whatever you want for yourself from the serving cart. You also will find a bottle of Remisier and a snifter there that you can serve to Mr. Hewitt. I am sure he will not refuse it."

"You are correct," Hewitt said with enthusiasm as Saul mixed himself a scotch on the rocks and delivered the cognac.

"Thank you both for coming," Wolfe said as he opened the first of two bottles of beer Fritz brought in. "I have reached a conclusion regarding the death of Mr. Breckenridge and the poisoning of Mr. Ennis."

"Really! And what is that conclusion?" Hewitt asked.

"Later," Wolfe said, holding up a hand. "I want all the members of the production's cast here, along with Mr. Sperry. Preferably the night after tomorrow."

"I can try," Hewitt said, "but I am not sure they will come, or at least not all of them."

"You can tell them I plan to reveal a murderer, and that there is a strong likelihood there will be a police presence. An absence on anyone's part would be seen as suspect."

"Who else will be here?" Saul asked.

"Besides you and Mr. Hewitt, I plan to invite Inspector Cramer."

"Where do I fit into all this?" I asked.

"We will get to that," Wolfe said. "Mr. Hewitt can start calling tomorrow morning." He then laid out detailed plans for one of what Cramer has referred to as "Wolfe's damned charades." The inspector may not like these sessions, but they invariably result in the identifying of a culprit.

This time, however, I was not so sure of success. I saw where Wolfe was heading, and I had finally begun to catch up, albeit belatedly, with his line of reasoning, and maybe you have, too. But I thought the scenario he laid out was shaky at best and filled with potential pitfalls. I did not have a better idea though, so I was hardly in a position to complain.

# CHAPTER 30

The next morning at 10:15, I answered a call from Lewis Hewitt. "Here is the rundown, Archie," he said. "I got lucky in one respect, and I managed to reach everyone Mr. Wolfe wants to have at the brownstone tomorrow night. I was not so fortunate in getting them all to agree, however."

"Okay, give me the news, both good and bad."

"The good first: Brad Lester, Steve Peters, and Melissa Cartwright all agreed to come without a great deal of complaining. Brad seemed a little irritated, Steve said he would postpone a dinner with his agent, and Melissa told me she couldn't understand why were having such a meeting, but that she would show up."

"And the rest?"

"Believe it or not, the individual I thought would be the most difficult to persuade, Ashley Williston, actually agreed to be present, but she was not the least bit happy about it, and she made that crystal clear to me. 'I am only doing this out of respect for Roy,' she said, 'but I believe it to be nothing more or less than an ego trip for Mr. Nero Wolfe, who obviously has an insatiable hunger for publicity.'"

"An interesting comment from one who has her own insatiable hunger for publicity. Mark her down as less than delighted," I said. "You have not mentioned Hollis Sperry or Teresa Reed."

"For good reason. They both flatly refuse to be a party to this show. Sperry told me he thought the idea of a mass gathering was 'just plain stupid' and that it would not accomplish a thing. And Teresa Reed said she was insulted at having been asked. By the way, Archie, is Mr. Wolfe on the line with you?"

"No, it is just me."

"Good. Here is what Mrs. Reed said: 'If the police have not gotten anywhere, why does that fat, pompous, and egomaniacal detective think that he can get anywhere? Let him put on his sham trial; I will not be there. The man is nothing more than a mountebank.'"

"Wolfe has been called all of that and worse," I said. "How did you leave things with our two recalcitrants?"

"I told them both that they would undoubtedly be hearing from Mr. Wolfe or someone from his office."

"Good. We will get back to you. Consider us set for tomorrow night unless you hear otherwise."

When Wolfe came down from the plant rooms and rang for beer, I filled him in.

"Call Saul," he said. I did, and he answered on the first ring. "Mr. Wolfe is on with me," I told him.

"Here is the situation," Wolfe said. "All but two of our guests have agreed to come tomorrow. Mr. Sperry and Mrs. Reed have refused the invitation. I want you to visit each of them and apply a combination of reason and pressure. Normally, this would be a job for Archie, but under the circumstances, such is clearly impossible. However, I trust you to be every bit as persuasive as our Mr. Goodwin. Lewis Hewitt knows where they can be reached. Archie, give Saul his telephone number."

I did, and Saul said, "Do not worry; they both will be at your place tomorrow if I have to put leashes on them and drag them along behind me. I will call later to confirm their attendance."

"I like his style," I told Wolfe, who turned back to his book, apparently satisfied that the situation was in hand.

At 4:15, I answered the phone in the office. "They both will be at the brownstone tomorrow night," Saul said.

"Do we want to know just how you accomplished this?"

"It was not as hard as you might think. I visited Sperry first. He has got a nicely furnished three-room flat on East Eighty-Fifth Street in Yorkville. At first, he did not want to let me in, but I wore him down by saying he should at the very least hear me out. We sat in his living room, and I told him that he was the only one who had refused to see Mr. Wolfe.

"That surprised him. He said 'Do you mean Ashley has really agreed to be part of this nonsense?' I made it clear to him that she did not object. Of course I had not mentioned Teresa Reed's resistance, but I figured that what he didn't know would not hurt him. Finally, he threw up his hands and said he would be there, but he made it clear that he didn't like it."

"Nice job. Was the cantankerous Mrs. Reed more difficult to persuade?"

"What do you think, Archie? She and her husband have

a cozy place in a four-story walkup on Bedford Street in the Village. As you recall, her husband is the house manager at one of the Broadway theaters, and he was at work, overseeing a matinee. She refused to let me in, so we ended up jawing out in the hall. I told her—this time it was the truth—that she was the only holdout among the *Cresthaven* bunch, and that her absence would be seen as extremely questionable behavior.

"'What do I care if it seems questionable?' she snapped at me. 'If that Wolfe character doesn't like it, he knows exactly what he can do. Nobody is ever going to tell me where I have to be or what I have to do.' I then played the card I had hoped to avoid, Archie: I told her it was very likely that a member of the police department would be present and would surely be intrigued by her absence.'"

"How did she react to that?"

"At first, she acted—and I do mean acted—as if she did not give a damn who was going to be there, but I saw that her resistance was beginning to weaken, so I moved in for the kill, so to speak. 'If you are guilty of killing Roy Breckenridge,' I told her, 'by all means, you should stay away from the meeting. The police will come calling on you soon enough. And if you are innocent, why not show up and find out who the murderer is?'"

"You must have majored in psychology somewhere along the way," I told Saul. "What did she say to that?"

"For several seconds, she just stood there in that dim hallway, her face screwed up and her hands on what passes for her hips. Finally, she sighed as if shouldering the world's burdens and allowed as to how she would make every effort to be there."

"Do you think she will show?"

"No doubt about it. I'd lay ten to one."

"I don't recall you throwing odds like that around very often."

"Archie, in the unlikely event that the woman does not make an appearance tomorrow night, I will go down to the Village and bring her back, forcibly if necessary."

"Better watch out. She seems like the type who could be a tigress."

"Maybe, but despite my size, I have been known to get somewhat fierce myself."

"I do not doubt it for a minute. But as you know, I abhor violence in all but extreme cases."

"I certainly do. I promise that I will try to restrain myself and not rough up the lady too much."

"Thank you for that. By the way, the next time I see you, once again you won't see me."

"Not immediately, anyway. But the evening promises to be an interesting one, doesn't it?"

"Yeah, I can hardly wait."


When Wolfe came down from the plant rooms at six, I summarized the events of the afternoon. After ringing for beer, he said, "Satisfactory. Get Inspector Cramer."

"He may have gone home. After all, he does have a life."

"Try him at work first, and then, if necessary, at his home."

I was spared the second call in a week to the Cramer household when the inspector answered his office phone and barked his last name. I nodded to Wolfe, who picked up his instrument and identified himself.

"Lord, now what?" Cramer demanded.

"I have invited the members of the cast of *Death at Cresthaven* to my home tomorrow night, sir, along with the production's stage manager. I propose to identify the individual who poisoned Roy Breckenridge. I felt you might want to be present. We will gather at nine."

Silence followed for thirty seconds, ending with a prolonged exhale. "Care to tell me who you have fingered?" Cramer asked in a tense tone.

"I do not, sir. That must wait until tomorrow."

"Of course it must. Ever the showman, aren't you?" Cramer fumed. "When in doubt, be as dramatic as possible. You have all the makings of a good Broadway director."

"I doubt that," Wolfe replied. "In such a role, I would be far too demanding for the tastes of the players, and in the process, I would surely bruise a great many fragile egos."

"I won't argue that. You don't exactly have a light touch, do you?"

"I did not call you so we could exchange verbal fusillades, sir. I felt it both honorable and respectful to extend an invitation. If you do not want to accept, that certainly is your prerogative."

Another extended pause. "I will be there, and I will be bringing Sergeant Stebbins with me."

"He is, of course, welcome to be present," Wolfe said evenly, although he was not expressing my feelings. Purley Stebbins and I have a long history, as I alluded to previously, and it is not a history I care to dwell upon.

# CHAPTER 31

As is always the case when Wolfe is about to stage one of his shows, my day moved very slowly, and I invariably found myself on edge. When I sat that morning at my table in the kitchen eating ham and scrambled eggs and reading the *New York Times*, Fritz hovered over me like a mother hen minus the clucking. "He seems much better today, Archie. When I took his breakfast and his *Times* up to him, he actually chuckled about something on the front page. *Chuckled!*"

"The worst is over," I told him. "You probably know we are having visitors tonight, including the police."

"I had guessed as much," Fritz said. "I know his moods, and sometimes I feel that I know what he is thinking."

"I am not surprised. You have that kind of sensitivity."

"Are you all right, Archie?" he asked, concern etched on his face.

"Of course. Why do you ask?"

"These days when he . . . when he does his—what do you call it?—his deductions, they are hard for you, aren't they?"

"I didn't realize it showed. But yes, it is the waiting all those hours that gets to me. None of this bothers him in the least, though. He behaves as if this is just an ordinary day filled with beer, books, crossword puzzles, and orchids—and your superb meals, of course."

Fritz turned away to begin working on one of those superb meals while I read every article on page one of the *Times* and tried to figure out what it was that made Wolfe chuckle.

After breakfast, I took a cup of coffee into the office and polished off some correspondence Wolfe had dictated the day before, placing it in a neat stack on his desk for signing. I looked for something else to occupy my time, but finally got reduced to cleaning off my typewriter with the little brush that came with it. That took care of a whole twenty minutes. I had lugged five shirts and a suit to the cleaners just yesterday, so they would not yet be ready to be picked up. The orchid germination records were current, and all the bills had been paid.

I was reduced to taking a walk, hardly an imposition on a sunny August morning in Manhattan. Because my last stroll had taken me west to the Hudson, this time I went in the opposite direction, across town toward the East River. As often as I have prowled the streets, avenues, and byways of this old Dutch island, I invariably learn something new each time.

On a block in the East Forties that I had traversed many times, I became aware of a narrow storefront I had not previously been drawn to. It was a model railroad store in which two electric trains in the front window operated on tracks that ran through a miniature town complete with trees, stores, a barbershop, a factory, a mountain with a tunnel, and a depot. As a kid back in Ohio, I had a model train that ran in a loop under our Christmas tree, but it was nowhere near as elaborate as this.

Intrigued, I stepped inside and was greeted by a short, bald man wearing a vest over an open-collared shirt. "Greetings, is there anything that I can interest you in, young man?" he said, peering over rimless glasses that had settled halfway down his ruddy nose.

"I was just passing by and noticed those trains running in your window. Very impressive. Has this store been here long?"

He laughed. "In fact, I opened up shop almost nine years back, but until a month ago, I had never put an operating layout in the window. It has done wonders for my business, I can tell you. I was a fool for not thinking of it earlier. Fortunately for me, it is never too late to learn."

The proprietor then regaled me with a series of stories about the joys of owning model trains. He even tried, without success, to sell me an engine that he said was a scale model reproduction of the steam locomotive that had hauled the Twentieth Century Limited, the luxury train Lily had once ridden with friends to see an opera in Chicago.

I finally disentangled myself from the verbal grip of the eager and enthusiastic shopkeeper, but when I stepped out onto the street, I realized that for the last half hour or more, I had not once thought about tonight's activities. I headed back to the brownstone feeling rejuvenated and ready for whatever awaited.


With Wolfe out of his funk and back at work, Fritz bustled around with enthusiasm, preparing lunch, planning for dinner, and making sure the liquor cart in the office was well stocked for the evening's visitors. I assumed Theodore had perked up as well, now that Wolfe was back on his schedule up in the plant rooms.

At eight thirty, as planned, Saul and Lewis Hewitt arrived, and the four of us went over the evening's program. Wolfe was unusually amiable, while Hewitt expressed concern about the presence of Cramer and Stebbins, and Saul exhibited what I would call guarded optimism.

"Mr. Cramer will no doubt play the curmudgeon," Wolfe said, "as is invariably the case during these sessions. But I would not be overly concerned about his behavior. This is part and parcel of who the man is. You cannot change his stripes, and it would be folly to attempt such."

At that moment, the doorbell rang. The evening had begun.

# CHAPTER 32

Wolfe left the office for the kitchen, Saul went to the front door, Hewitt remained in the red leather chair usually reserved for the client, and I took my post in the alcove for one last time.

Cramer and Stebbins arrived first, both lumbering into the office looking like they could chew nails by the bucketful. "Oh, you're . . . Hewitt, right?" Cramer asked, skidding to a stop. "Where the hell is Wolfe? Oh, never mind, I know," he said, slapping his forehead with a palm. "He likes to make a grand entry." Purley Stebbins sneered but said nothing. He has always excelled at sneering. If either of them wondered where I was, they did not remark on it.

The bell rang again, and Saul was off once more to play doorman. He returned with Teresa Reed, who wore her own brand of a sneer. "You, you're the top cop, right?" she said, pointing a bony index finger at Cramer. "What are you doing here, or shouldn't I ask?"

"I am the top cop only in the Homicide Division, Mrs. Reed," Cramer said, showing remarkable reserve. "I am present as an observer. And this is Sergeant Stebbins."

"Observer, hah! Don't give me that nonsense. You are really here to make a pinch, and I will bet the one you pinch is that phony Canadian magazine writer. What I would like to know is why you let that Nero Wolfe do your work for you?"

Cramer's face turned as red as the inside of one of Rusterman's rare filets, but he said nothing.

By now, the doorbell was getting a workout. Saul brought in a grim-faced Hollis Sperry, then a timid-appearing Melissa Cartwright and a smiling Brad Lester, the latter making a snappy entry and seeming outwardly happy to be present. Steve Peters was right behind him, shooting the cuffs on his sport coat and looking as though he would rather be somewhere else. Then, after an interval of at least three minutes, the bell rang yet again. Saul escorted Ashley Williston in, and the first lady of the American stage, at least in her own mind, showed even Lester how to make an entry, looking left and then right, one arm out in a general greeting. She probably had been across the street in a taxi or maybe a limo, making sure all the others had entered before her. She was clad in a black sheath and black patent pumps, and she wore a string of pearls that looked like the real McCoy.

Saul was the picture of efficiency, seating our guests as planned: The women occupied the front row, Melissa seated nearest to Saul, who would be at my desk, then Ashley in the middle and Teresa Reed on her right.

The second row of chairs had Steve Peters on the left, Lester in the middle, and Sperry on the right. Cramer and Stebbins sat in the third row but both looked like they were ready to spring. Saul went behind Wolfe's desk and reached under it to push the buzzer.

Wolfe walked in, detoured around his desk, and sat, surveying the assemblage. "Thank you all for coming," he said. "I do not believe it necessary to tell you why you are here."

"What I don't get is why *they* are here," Hollis Sperry rasped, turning in his chair and jabbing a thumb in the direction of Cramer and Stebbins.

"They are Inspector—"

"I know damned well who they are, you don't have to tell me!" the stage manager shot back. "I have been questioned, more than once I might add, and I am damned sick of it."

"I believe there will be no more mass interrogations after this evening," Wolfe said. "As to the presence of the police, these gentlemen are present at my invitation and remain at my sufferance. Does any one of you object?" He looked at each of the six, none of whom spoke.

"Very well. Would anyone like liquid refreshments? Mr. Panzer will serve you."

"Drinks at a time like this? What utter nonsense," Teresa Reed sputtered. "This is not a cocktail party, unless I have been badly misled."

"I don't know about anyone else, but I could use something," Sperry said. "I'll have scotch on the rocks. From my last visit here, I know you pour a top-notch label of the stuff."

"Mr. Sperry's endorsement is all that I need to hear," Brad Lester said. "I will have what he's having."

Saul looked around, but there were no other takers, so he went to the serving cart to pour two scotches while Fritz slipped in with beer for the host.

"I realize this is the second time each of you has been here," Wolfe said, "and I appreciate your patience."

"It is so nice to know we are appreciated, Mr. Wolfe," Ashley Williston said in a stage voice oozing sarcasm, "but I find this gathering to be totally unnecessary. I believe everyone in this room knows the scenario: Poor Max Ennis, for whatever reason, poisoned Roy and then tried to take his own life."

"Nonsense!" Teresa Reed spat. "I simply do not understand why everyone in this room, and I include the police, seems to avoid discussing that so-called magazine writer from what has proven to be a fictional Canadian arts magazine. Tell me why it is so difficult to locate this individual."

Wolfe considered her and spoke. "Mrs. Reed has a valid point. The time has come to bring Mr. Alan MacGregor into the picture." He ran a finger along one side of his nose, my cue to enter the stage.

And what an entry it was. As I stepped into the office, every face swiveled toward me.

"That is him, that's the one!" Teresa shrieked, standing. "I knew that this guy was a phony from the start. His answers were much too pat when I asked him why he didn't have a Canadian accent and where he was from."

"Where has he been hiding all this time?" Brad Lester asked. Now everyone was on their feet, and most of them were talking over one another.

"So now we have our man," Ashley Williston said, clapping her hands and turning toward Cramer. "Arrest him."

"Enough!" Wolfe said. "The individual all of you know to be Alan MacGregor is my longtime associate, Archie Goodwin. Now, will everyone please be seated?"

"Mister, you have got plenty of explaining to do over this," Hollis Sperry said with his trademark scowl.

"Which I will," Wolfe replied as everyone quieted down and got settled. "Roy Breckenridge came to me seeking my aid in identifying the cause of what he said was a miasma that seemed to be permeating the atmosphere around his production. He and I devised a stratagem whereby Mr. Goodwin would pose as a magazine writer in an attempt to discover the source of this taint."

"In other words, he was a spy," Ashley said.

"If you choose," Wolfe said.

"And MacGregor, or rather, Goodwin, was not successful in his assignment, was he?" Sperry said.

"No, sir, he was not. Obviously, his work was cut short by the death of Mr. Breckenridge."

"Just what was the cause of this—what did you call it—miasma?" Lester asked.

"Ah, now we come to the crux of the matter, and to my own lack of perspicacity," Wolfe said.

"What the God's name is all that supposed to mean?" Sperry demanded.

"Mr. Breckenridge was not altogether candid and forthcoming when he came to me for help," Wolfe said. "He was more than a little vague as to the essence of the unease he claimed was permeating the production, but it is to my shame that I did not press him for specifics. Had I done so, he likely would be alive today. However, it was only after his death that it became apparent the threat was not some vague aura hovering over the theater, but rather a most specific threat to the man himself."

"Will you please get to the point?" Ashley Williston urged. "It appears obvious to me, and probably to the others here, that you like to hear yourself talk, but it is possible that we are not enamored of your voice."

"It is always helpful to be reminded of one's foibles, madam, and I will take your comments into consideration," Wolfe said. "As I started to say before you chose to admonish me, the police discovered some notes in Mr. Breckenridge's home after his death."

"Three to be exact," Cramer said, "printed with ink in block letters on plain stationery with no fingerprints except Mr. Breckenridge's own."

"The contents of all three messages were essentially the same," Wolfe went on. "One read 'If you do not cease with your sinful behavior, you will pay and pay dearly.' The others were almost identical."

"Pretty dramatic stuff," Lester observed with a nervous laugh.

"Melodramatic," Wolfe corrected. "As I said, the other two missives contained essentially the same message. It is fair to say they unnerved Mr. Breckenridge."

"So they were sent to him by his killer," Sperry said.

"They were not," Wolfe demurred.

"So is it possible that Mr. Breckenridge sent them to himself?" Melissa asked.

"No, it is not."

"Then just who did write these nasty little notes, or do you even know that?" Teresa Reed demanded.

"I do, madam. It was Max Ennis."

"Wait a minute," Brad Lester said. "You are telling us that Ennis wrote threatening notes but that he did not kill Roy?"

"Precisely."

"That makes no sense at all."

"He has got a point," Cramer said. "If you are actually going somewhere with all of this, can't you speed it along?"

"I will try to be more expeditious, sir."

"Please do," Ashley said. "I am glad to hear you say that Max, gentle soul that he is, did not kill Roy. But how do you explain those notes?"

"Mr. Ennis, who remains comatose, did not poison Roy Breckenridge, although he made it seem so by his own message, which was found in his apartment."

"The one that read 'I'm sorry.' That much was in the newspapers," Ashley said. "So if Max did not poison Roy, why did he make it seem like that was the case with that 'I'm sorry' note?"

"I am getting to that, madam. I had conversations with each of you, individually, in this room. And—"

"Oh, we are all too aware of that," Sperry said. "Did one of us say something that led you to who you believe to be guilty?"

"Rather, it was something *not* said that I found significant, although I failed to pick up on it at the time."

"Proving once again that none of us is perfect," Teresa said with a sour smile.

Wolfe ignored her. "Only one individual did not inquire as to the condition of Mr. Ennis, and that person also neglected to ask anything about Mr. MacGregor's whereabouts."

"I guess I just do not . . . do not see your point," Steve Peters said.

"My point is that the individual in question evinced a marked lack of curiosity, and also a lack of concern for Mr. Ennis. Yet it was precisely because of Max's own concern for this person that he behaved as he did—ingesting the same poison that killed Mr. Breckenridge and writing that note, both actions that were designed to point to him as the killer. One might term such behavior a noble sacrifice."

"But a sacrifice for whom?" Lester asked.

"For Miss Cartwright, of course," Wolfe said, turning toward Melissa, who made a gasping sound, sliding down in her chair and starting to sniffle.

"This is a ridiculous accusation!" Peters said, surprised at the loudness of his words. "Melissa had no reason whatever to dislike Mr. Breckenridge. He had given her a wonderful opportunity."

"But that opportunity came with a price, and to her, a very

steep price," Wolfe said. "It is common knowledge in the theater community that Roy Breckenridge was strongly drawn to attractive women. He—"

"That is putting it mildly, as a lot of us are all too aware," Teresa interrupted.

"He was making demands upon Miss Cartwright, demands she chose not to accede to. So she took steps to remove him from the production."

"But not to kill him," Melissa said, now racked with sobs as Purley Stebbins moved beside her. I almost—but not quite—felt sorry for her.

"I put what I thought was a small dose of arsenic into his Coca-Cola, just enough to . . . to get him out of the way during the rest of the play's run," Melissa continued. "I . . . had no intention whatever of . . . of . . ."

"What total idiocy!" Ashley Williston said, standing and turning to the younger woman. "Here we have an amateur practicing with poison. Or did you have some previous experience?"

"So was Max going to take the fall for her?" Sperry asked.

"He was, and willingly," Wolfe said. "Mr. Ennis had become Miss Cartwright's confidant, perhaps even a father figure, as has been suggested. And when Mr. Breckenridge was poisoned, Mr. Ennis realized immediately what had transpired and set out to protect Miss Cartwright from punishment. It was a somewhat clumsy effort, but he did not care. He knew that because of his health, his time was running out, so he decided that a suicide would both end his own pain and free Miss Cartwright from suspicion."

"Ah, but what possible motive would Ennis have for killing Breckenridge?" Sperry asked. "They had always gotten along well and respected each other. On several occasions over the years, Roy had gone out of his way to praise Max to me as a consummate professional."

"Miss Cartwright tried to create a reason for enmity between the two," Wolfe said. "She claimed she overheard them in a heated argument after a performance. But no one else connected with the production said they had heard or been aware of such a dispute. And as has been pointed out, the theater occupies a tightly contained space, and the walls between dressing rooms are thin. Any loud discussion would surely have been heard by several persons."

Cramer had heard enough. He stepped forward, joining Stebbins. "Melissa Cartwright, I am arresting you on suspicion of the murder of Roy Breckenridge. You have the right to remain silent. Anything you say or do can be—"

"I know, I know . . . You are reading that Miranda warning," she said in a barely audible tone, punctuated by more weeping. "I know exactly what it is; it was used in a play I performed in at Michigan State. I will go with you." She turned to the others. "I am sorry, so sorry, so very sorry." She got to her feet with what seemed like great effort and walked out, head down, led by the grim-faced Cramer and Stebbins, neither of whom spoke.

# CHAPTER 33

After the departure of Melissa and the police, the room was silent, as if everyone were in shock, which may have been the case.

"I would not have believed this," Brad Lester said, finally breaking the silence. "She seemed so . . . innocent, I guess, is the word I would have used to describe her."

"Huh! I knew very well that she was not as naive as she appeared," Teresa Reed said. "Women are better at spotting these things than men, a lot better. But still, I never would have guessed at . . . this."

"If you all will excuse me," Wolfe said, rising, "I have another engagement." He walked out of the office, probably heading for the kitchen. Not one for small talk, he saw no reason to remain in a room with these people.

Everyone was on their feet again. "Well, how do you feel about *your* performance?" Ashley Williston asked me. "Doesn't it give you a guilty conscience to have taken part in that masquerade?"

"The only thing I feel guilty about," I told her, "is that I was not able to prevent what happened. I will have to live with the knowledge that I, like Mr. Wolfe, did not realize how real the danger was to our client."

"There are people who would say he deserved what he got," Teresa said. "I realize that sounds harsh, and if so, I apologize."

"Roy Breckenridge will go down in the books as one of Broadway's greatest producers and directors," Hollis Sperry said. "As to his behavior in other areas . . ." He shrugged and shook his head.

"This has been a black day," Lewis Hewitt said. "Three members of the *Cresthaven* family are casualties. One dead, one arrested, one on life support and very possibly near death."

"And it is probably the end of the production, although that seems unimportant at the moment," Lester put in.

"Well I, for one, am sorry to see things come to an end this way," Ashley Williston said as though she were speaking lines to a standing-room-only theater. "I am sure many of our paths will cross again." With that, she swept out regally on clicking heels with Saul following her to the front door.

"I have to be honest, Mr. Goodwin," Lester said. "I was disappointed to learn who you really were. But I suppose I can understand why you did what you did. I am just damned sorry that you couldn't have prevented what happened."

"No sorrier than I am, I assure you of that. There were no winners at all that I can see in this real-life performance."

One by one, the remaining guests trickled out, each exchanging a few words with Hewitt, whom they all seemed to like. I received no such farewells, which was understandable. To them, I was definitely a Caleb, no matter the intent of my deception. After all of them had left the brownstone, I dialed Lon Cohen, having earlier suggested he remain in his office until he heard from me. He was to get his scoop after all.

# CHAPTER 34

Melissa Cartwright never was able to return home to Lansing in an attempt to get her parents reconciled. But she did dodge the murder rap, thanks to the brilliant and high-powered Manhattan trial lawyer her father, the Oldsmobile marketing executive, had retained for her defense. The smooth-talking mouthpiece copped an insanity plea, and Melissa played her part to the hilt as an unhinged woman, according to a *Gazette* reporter, who told Lon that "she earned her Tony right there in the courtroom. And it did not hurt her cause that she dressed primly and managed to maintain a wide-eyed and dazed 'little me' innocence throughout the trial."

Her lawyer argued that she had become so distraught over her parents' impending divorce that she was sent spiraling into a form of derangement, and that she could not be held accountable for her subsequent actions. Amazingly, a court-appointed psychiatrist confirmed the diagnosis of the defense's own shrink, and the jury bought it, bringing back a quick verdict of guilt by reason of insanity.

Melissa resides at a state psychiatric facility in rolling farm country more than two hundred miles north of New York City, where, according to a *Gazette* feature writer who visited the place, "she spends much of her time organizing amateur theatrical productions for the patients, all of whom seem to thrive under her direction. She has become something of a celebrity at the institution, spinning yarns about her adventures on Broadway but avoiding the episode that ended her acting career."

After several weeks, Max Ennis regained consciousness and steadfastly refused to explain why he took the poison and left the infamous "I'm sorry" note or the three notes sent to Breckenridge. He denied having anything whatever to do with Roy Breckenridge's death and not once did he ask about Melissa Cartwright.

Given the fragile state of his health, Ennis never returned to the stage and eventually moved into a retirement home in Westchester County, where, until the end of his life, he was said to regale the other residents with tales of stage personalities he had known and performed with over his long career, much like what Melissa was doing to a lesser degree in her own institution to the north.

Hollis Sperry continues to toil as a demanding and crusty Broadway stage manager, and he told Lewis Hewitt recently that because of his years working with Roy Breckenridge, he has remained in demand with other directors, one of whom said, "If Roy kept asking for you on his productions, you have got to be good."

Teresa Reed reinvented herself as a television star of sorts. She managed to get herself cast as an eccentric and grouchy aunt in a popular daytime soap opera and earned herself an award. But her late-in-life success has by no means mellowed her. At the awards ceremony, she said, "It is about time I won something, for heaven's sake. I slaved for years on Broadway and never got so much as a pat on the head like a good dog. At least you folks know class when you see it."

Teresa is not the only *Death at Cresthaven* cast member who has been showered with honors. Brad Lester, who decided he liked Broadway after his brief stint in *Cresthaven*, was cast as Ezra in a restaging of Eugene O'Neill's *Mourning Becomes Electra* and won a Tony for Best Actor in a Revival. One can only imagine how Ashley Williston must feel about this.

As for Lester, the award has made him in demand to the extent that he has made New York his home. And according to Lily Rowan, he has found himself a new companion, an extremely fetching raven-haired divorcée whom I have met at a couple of soirees at Lily's penthouse abode. "They make a very glamorous pairing," she told me, "and I would not be surprised if that pairing becomes permanent."

Speaking of Ashley Williston, the woman who likes to fancy herself as the next Helen Hayes, she lost any chance she had of winning a Tony when *Cresthaven* never reopened. Angry at a Broadway she felt never gave her the recognition she deserved, Ashley crossed the Atlantic and has made something of a name for herself on the British stage.

"It is marvelous to be where I am appreciated, and I think I have found a new home," she was quoted as saying in a *New York Times* article about her popularity with the British. She has appeared in two London dramas and has gotten generally positive reviews. It was even speculated that she might be in the running for a British theater award.

"We find Miss Williston to be a breath of fresh air on the

West End theatre scene. Over the years, we have sent so much acting talent to the States. It is refreshing to see that on a rare occasion, the Yanks reciprocate," wrote the critic for London's *Telegraph.*

Speaking some more of Ashley Williston, last week, Lewis Hewitt and I dined at Rusterman's Restaurant because of the bet we had made as to who got the better of it when Wolfe interviewed Ashley in the brownstone. I thought my boss was the winner, but Hewitt insisted on casting his vote for the actress. The result: We each bought our own meal.

"I am one of several backers of a new musical that is now in rehearsals," Hewitt told me over dessert. "And among its cast is none other than our own Steve Peters, who, as it turns out, has a very fine tenor voice. And the young man is an accomplished dancer as well."

"So our boy looks like he's in the world of greasepaint to stay," I said. "I am happy to hear it. He seems like a decent guy."

"And that is not all, Archie. I have seen him several times in the company of a most attractive young woman who drops by after almost every rehearsal, and off they go to heaven only knows where."

"Well, that is hardly a surprise, is it? He's pretty good-looking himself."

"True, but what makes this particularly interesting is that the lady in question bears a striking resemblance to Melissa Cartwright, red hair and all."

"Let us hope this relationship works out better for the young man than the previous one."

"Agreed. By the way, Archie, tell your boss he is to expect a package tomorrow morning."

"Dare I hazard a guess as to who it is from and what it contains?"

"I believe you know the answers to both questions," Hewitt said with a smile. "As I realize you are aware, Nero Wolfe can be one tough negotiator."

"Amen to that. I have had plenty of experience trying to get my salary bumped up. Over the years, we have had some interesting conversations on that subject."

I was at my desk with coffee the next morning at ten, updating the orchid germination records, when the front bell rang. I went to the door and, through the one-way glass, saw the tall, lean figure of Thursby, Lewis Hewitt's driver. In his black uniform and cap, the bright-eyed, square-jawed young man looked like Hollywood central casting's idea of the quintessential chauffeur. The large tray he was holding contained three tall packages covered in green paper that looked like something a florist would deliver.

"Good morning, Mr. Goodwin," he said as I opened the door. "I have something for Mr. Nero Wolfe from Mr. Hewitt."

"Come right in," I said to young Thursby. "Mr. Wolfe happens to be up in the plant rooms on the roof right now. May I give you a hand with those?"

"No, thank you, Mr. Goodwin, I can manage them."

"All right, then. I am sure he would be happy if you made the delivery to him in person." I led him to the elevator and up he went, descending ten minutes later and wearing a wide grin. I saw him out and went back to my desk, where I was paying the bills when Wolfe walked in at eleven.

"Good morning, Archie, did you sleep well?" he asked as he invariably does.

I replied that I had, and he settled in behind his desk, ringing for beer and riffling through the morning mail, which I had as usual stacked on his blotter. I turned back to my work, and there came a sound I was not used to hearing in the office.

Nero Wolfe was whistling.

# AUTHOR NOTES

As with my previous Nero Wolfe stories, I express my sincere thanks to Barbara Stout and Rebecca Stout Bradbury for their continued support. My thanks also go to Otto Penzler of Mysterious Press, to whom this book is dedicated, and to his associate Rob Hart, as well as to the enthusiastic team at Open Road Integrated Media and to my agent, Martha Kaplan.

I also want to thank my friend Eric Berg, a Renaissance man who has made his name in the fields of both law and the theater, for his helpful counsel on details surrounding both the onstage and backstage intricacies of a major dramatic production.

Four volumes have been particularly helpful to me in my attempts to emulate the wonderful world of Nero Wolfe and company that Rex Stout created over a four-decade period. They are: *Nero Wolfe of West Thirty-Fifth Street: The Life and Times of America's Largest Private Detective* by William S. Baring-Gould (The Viking Press, New York, 1968); *The Nero Wolfe Cookbook* by Rex Stout and the Editors of the Viking Press (Viking Press, New York, 1973); *The Brownstone House of Nero Wolfe* by Ken Darby as Told by Archie Goodwin (Little, Brown, Boston, 1983); and *Rex Stout: A Biography* by John McAleer (Little, Brown, Boston, 1977). The McAleer volume justly won an Edgar Award in the biography category from the Mystery Writers of America.

My most heartfelt thanks go to my wife, Janet, who for more than a half century has redefined the term *soul mate*. She has patiently tolerated my many moods and eccentricities with grace and good humor.

# ABOUT THE AUTHOR

Robert Goldsborough is an American author best known for continuing Rex Stout's famous Nero Wolfe series. Born in Chicago, he attended Northwestern University and upon graduation went to work for the Associated Press, beginning a lifelong career in journalism that would include long periods at the *Chicago Tribune* and *Advertising Age*.

While at the *Tribune*, Goldsborough began writing mysteries in the voice of Rex Stout, the creator of iconic sleuths Nero Wolfe and Archie Goodwin. Goldsborough's first novel starring Wolfe, *Murder in E Minor* (1986), was met with acclaim from both critics and devoted fans, winning a Nero Award from the Wolfe Pack. Ten more Wolfe mysteries followed, including

*Death on Deadline* (1987) and *Fade to Black* (1990). In 2005, Goldsborough published *Three Strikes You're Dead*, the first in an original series starring Chicago Tribune reporter Snap Malek. *Murder, Stage Left* (2017) is his most recent novel.

# THE NERO WOLFE MYSTERIES

FROM MYSTERIOUSPRESS.COM
AND OPEN ROAD MEDIA

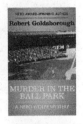

MYSTERIOUSPRESS.COM

Otto Penzler, owner of the Mysterious Bookshop in Manhattan, founded the Mysterious Press in 1975. Penzler quickly became known for his outstanding selection of mystery, crime, and suspense books, both from his imprint and in his store. The imprint was devoted to printing the best books in these genres, using fine paper and top dust-jacket artists, as well as offering many limited, signed editions.

Now the Mysterious Press has gone digital, publishing ebooks through **MysteriousPress.com**.

**MysteriousPress.com** offers readers essential noir and suspense fiction, hard-boiled crime novels, and the latest thrillers from both debut authors and mystery masters. Discover classics and new voices, all from one legendary source.

FIND OUT MORE AT

WWW.MYSTERIOUSPRESS.COM

FOLLOW US:

@emysteries and Facebook.com/MysteriousPressCom

MysteriousPress.com is one of a select group of publishing partners of Open Road Integrated Media, Inc.

**THe MYSTeRIouS BOOKSHOP**, founded in 1979, is located in Manhattan's Tribeca neighborhood. It is the oldest and largest mystery-specialty bookstore in America.

The shop stocks the finest selection of new mystery hardcovers, paperbacks, and periodicals. It also features a superb collection of signed modern first editions, rare and collectable works, and Sherlock Holmes titles. The bookshop issues a free monthly newsletter highlighting its book clubs, new releases, events, and recently acquired books.

58 Warren Street
info@mysteriousbookshop.com
(212) 587-1011
Monday through Saturday
11:00 a.m. to 7:00 p.m.

## FIND OUT MORE AT:

www.mysteriousbookshop.com

## FOLLOW US:

@TheMysterious and Facebook.com/MysteriousBookshop

INTEGRATED MEDIA

Find a full list of our authors and
titles at www.openroadmedia.com

FOLLOW US
@OpenRoadMedia